MARVEL GUARDIANS OF THE GALAXY DOODLES

Written by
Brandon T. Snider

Illustrated by
Tomás Montalvo-Lagos

Printed in the United States of America

First Edition, April 2017

10 9 8 7 6 5 4 3 2 1

ISBN 978-1-4847-8767-0

FAC-008598-17048

Library of Congress Control Number: 2016944546

Designed by Kurt Hartman

SUSTAINABLE FORESTRY INITIATIVE
Certified Sourcing
www.sfiprogram.org
SFI-00993
Logo Applies to Text Stock Only

MARVEL

Los Angeles
New York

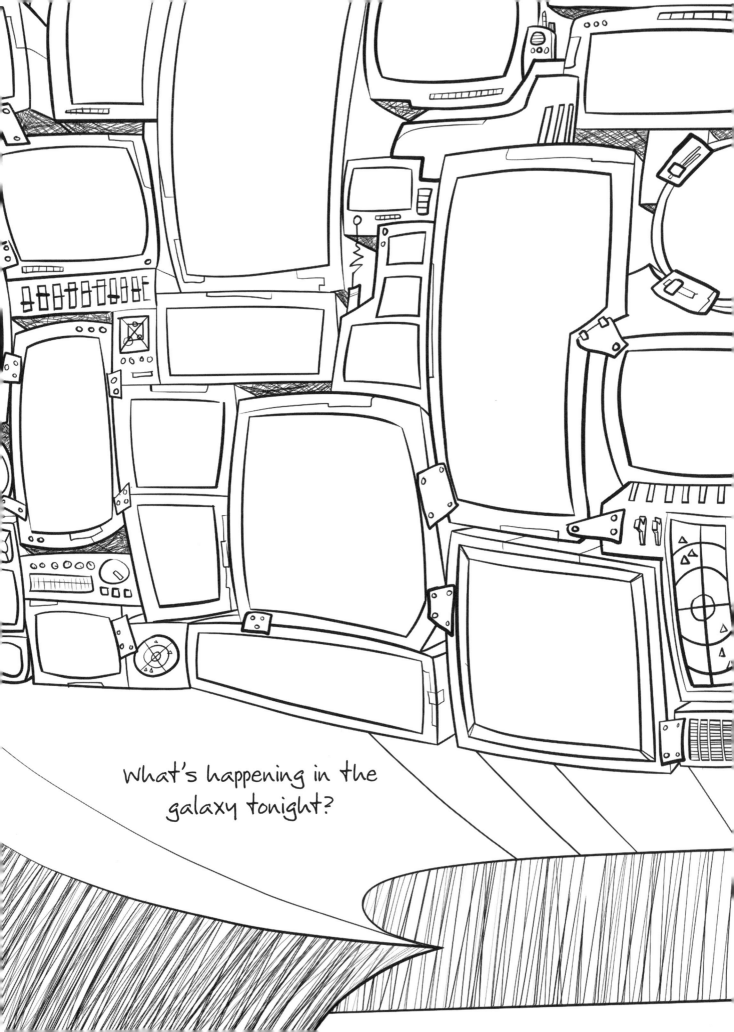

What's happening in the galaxy tonight?

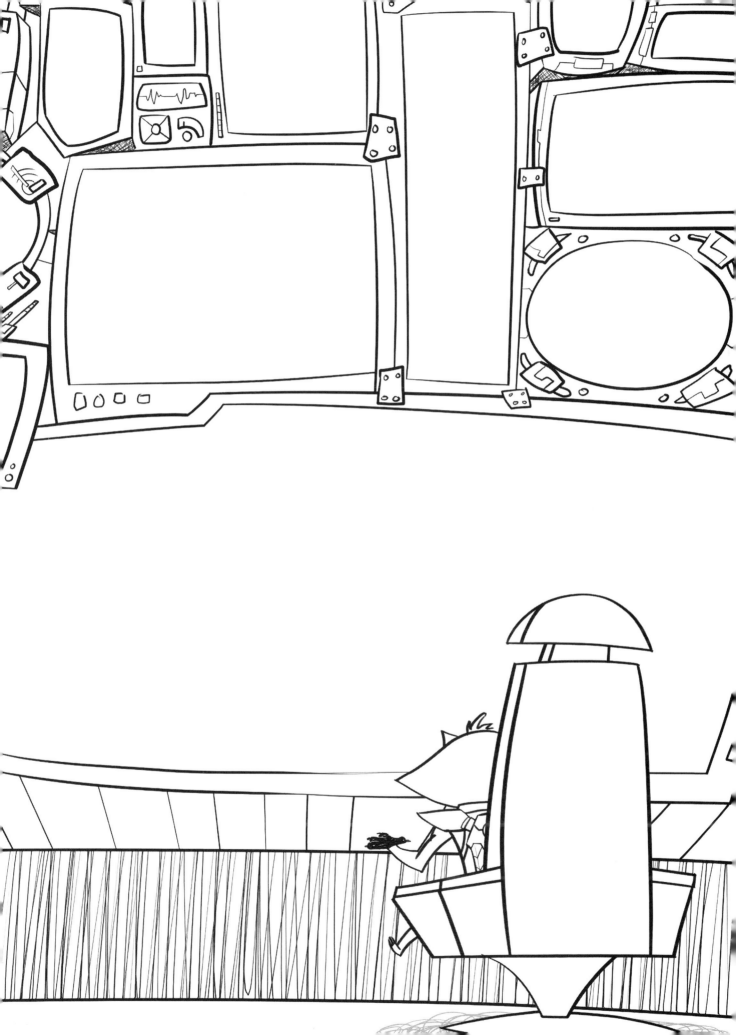

What the heck is Star-Lord thinking about?
Draw what you think is on his mind.

Which sword should Gamora
choose today?
Draw a bunch of options
for her to pick from.

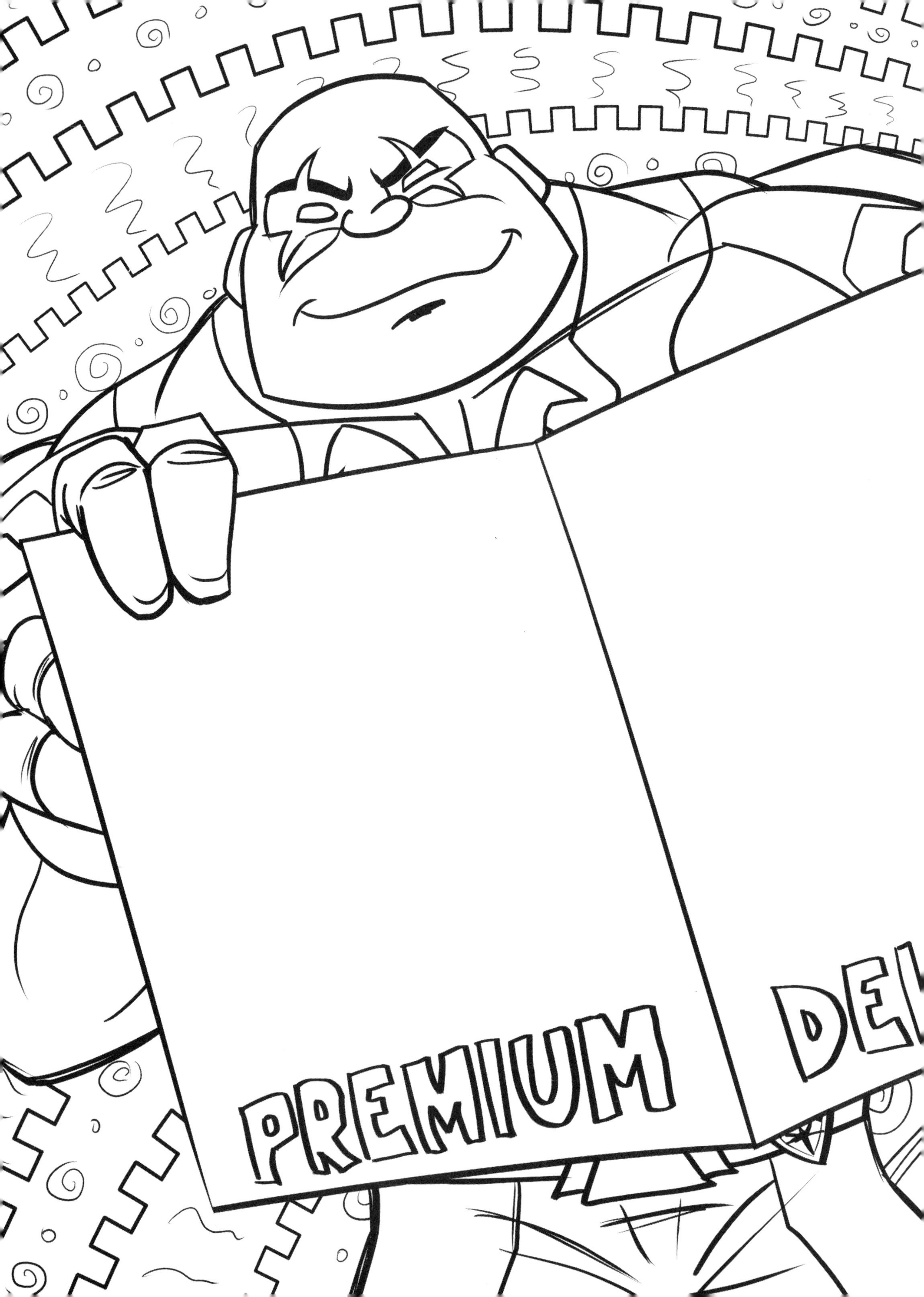
PREMIUM

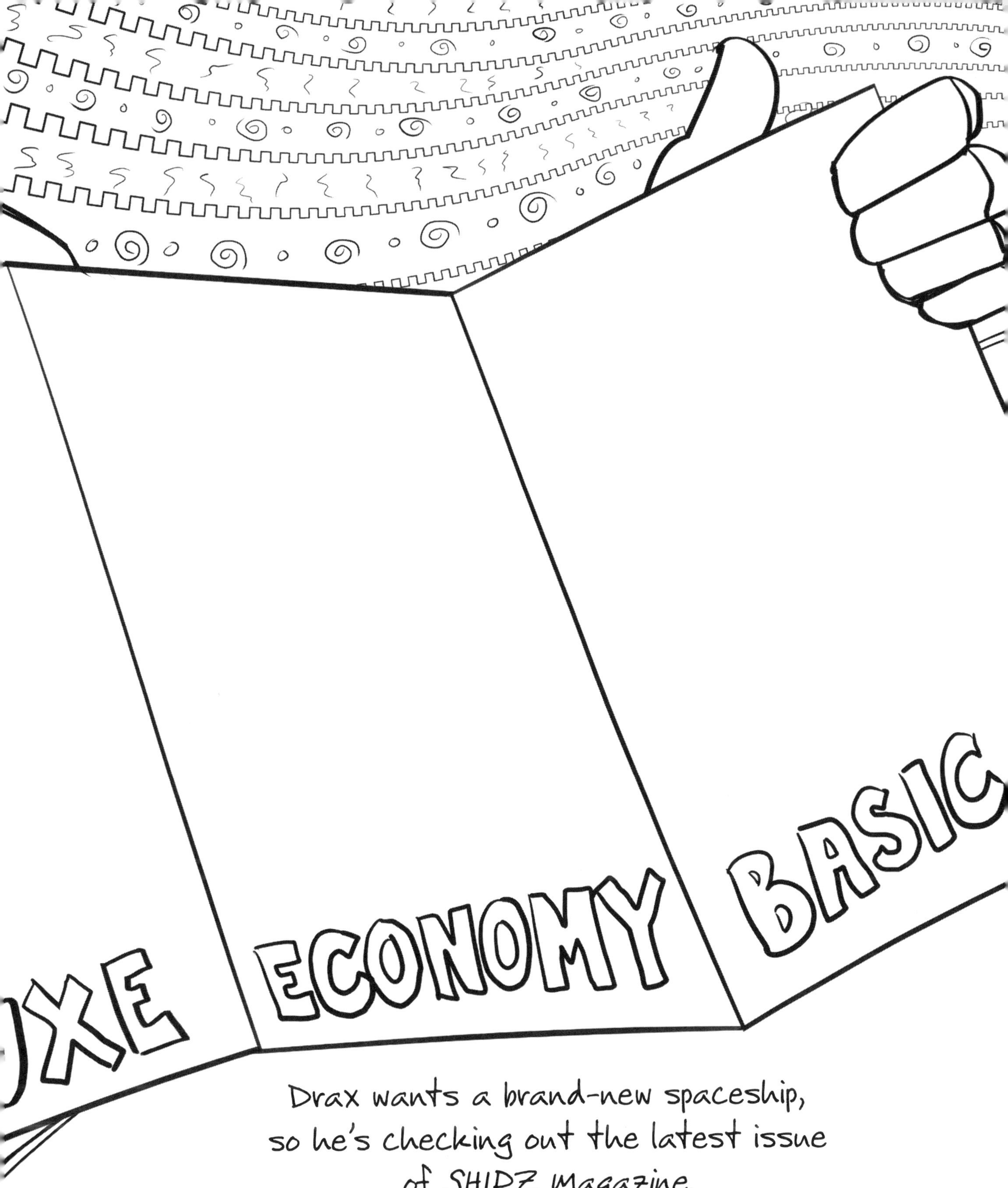
XE
ECONOMY
BASIC

Drax wants a brand-new spaceship,
so he's checking out the latest issue
of SHIPZ Magazine.
Draw some fancy (and not-so-fancy)
options for him to consider.

Decorate Groot like a holiday tree. Drape him in all kinds of lights and ornaments.

Oh, and don't forget to surround him with presents.

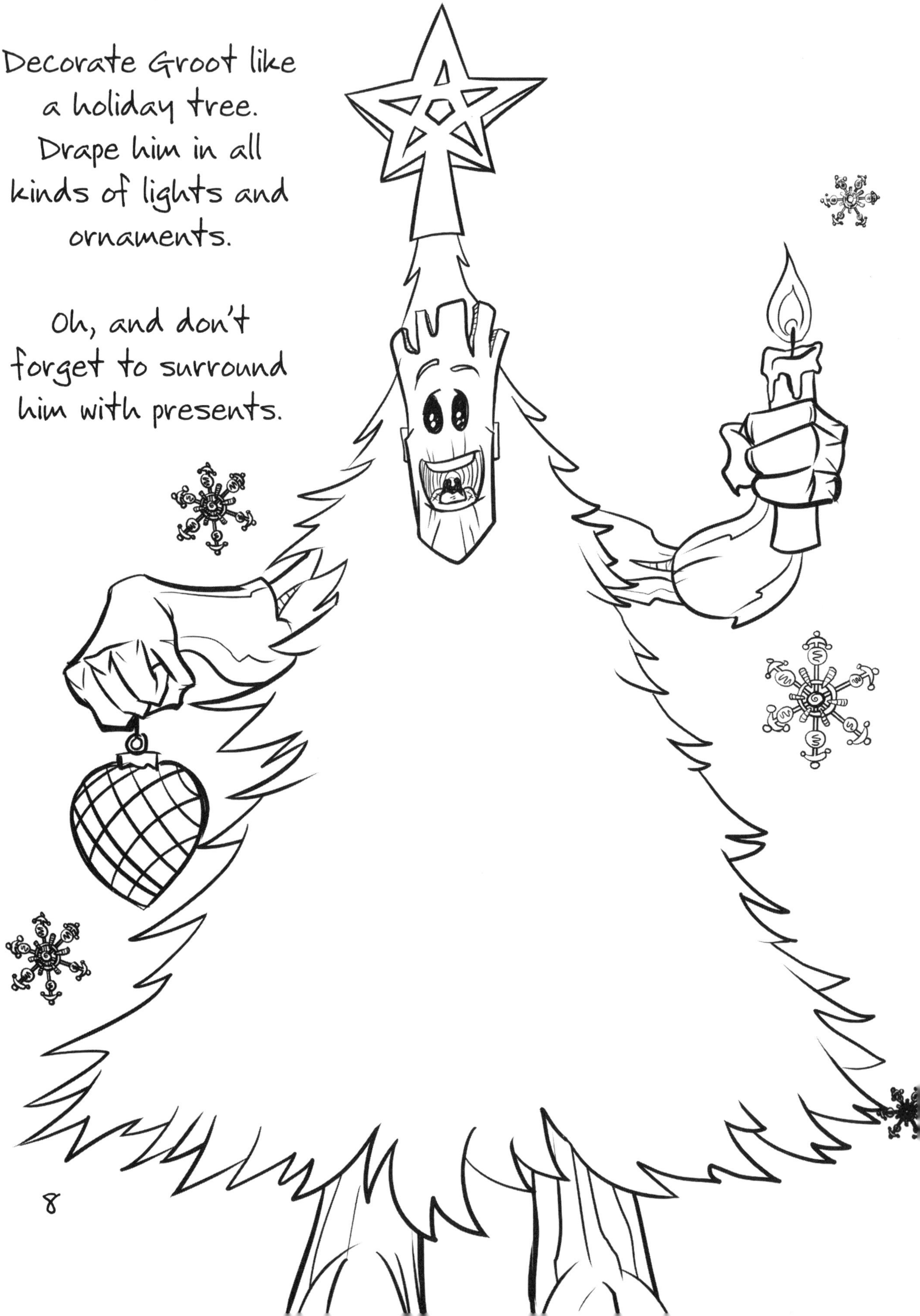

Yikes. Ronan the Accuser has a skull in his hand. Make it less creepy by covering it in colorful designs. Or makeup! That could be funny.

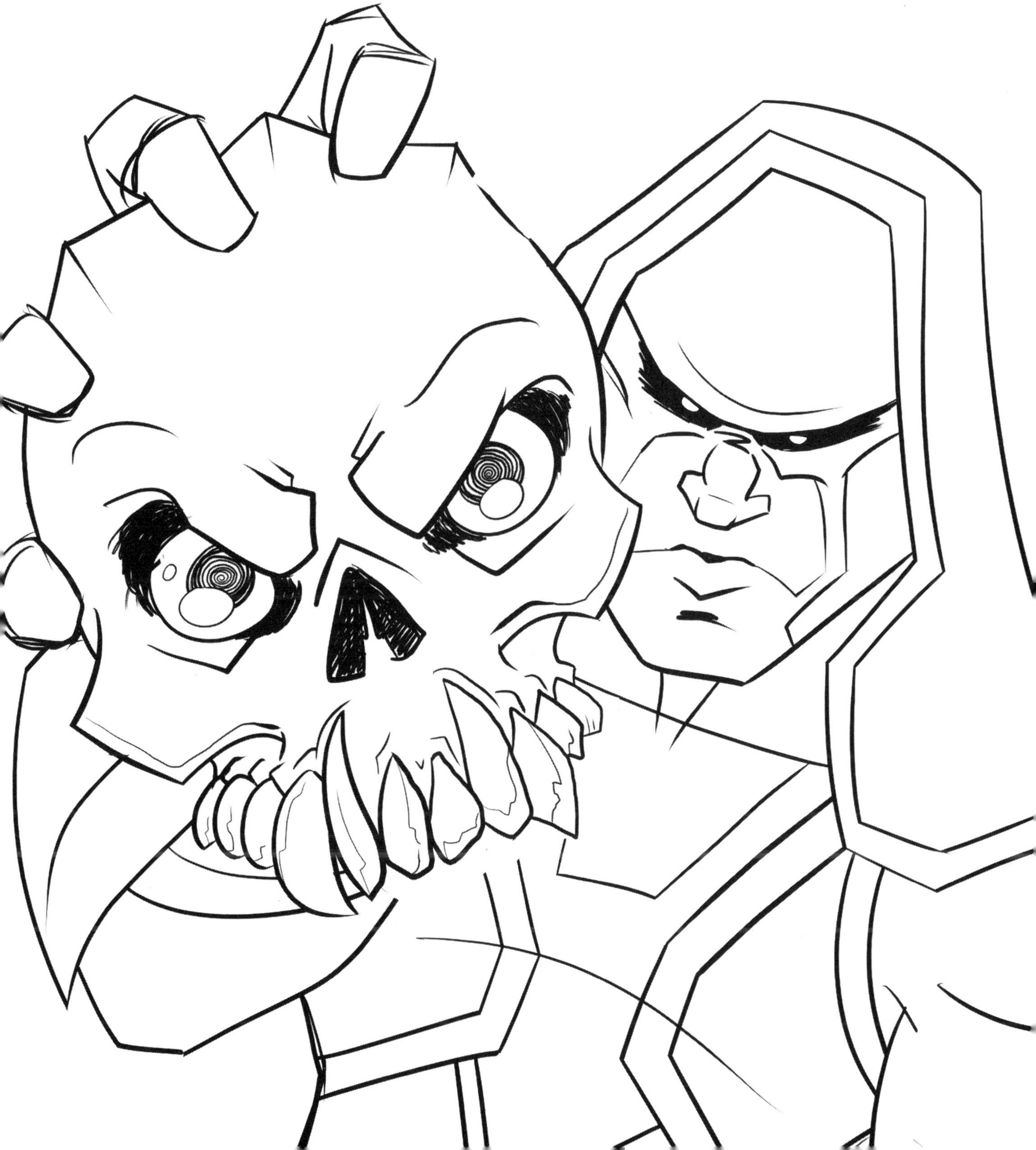

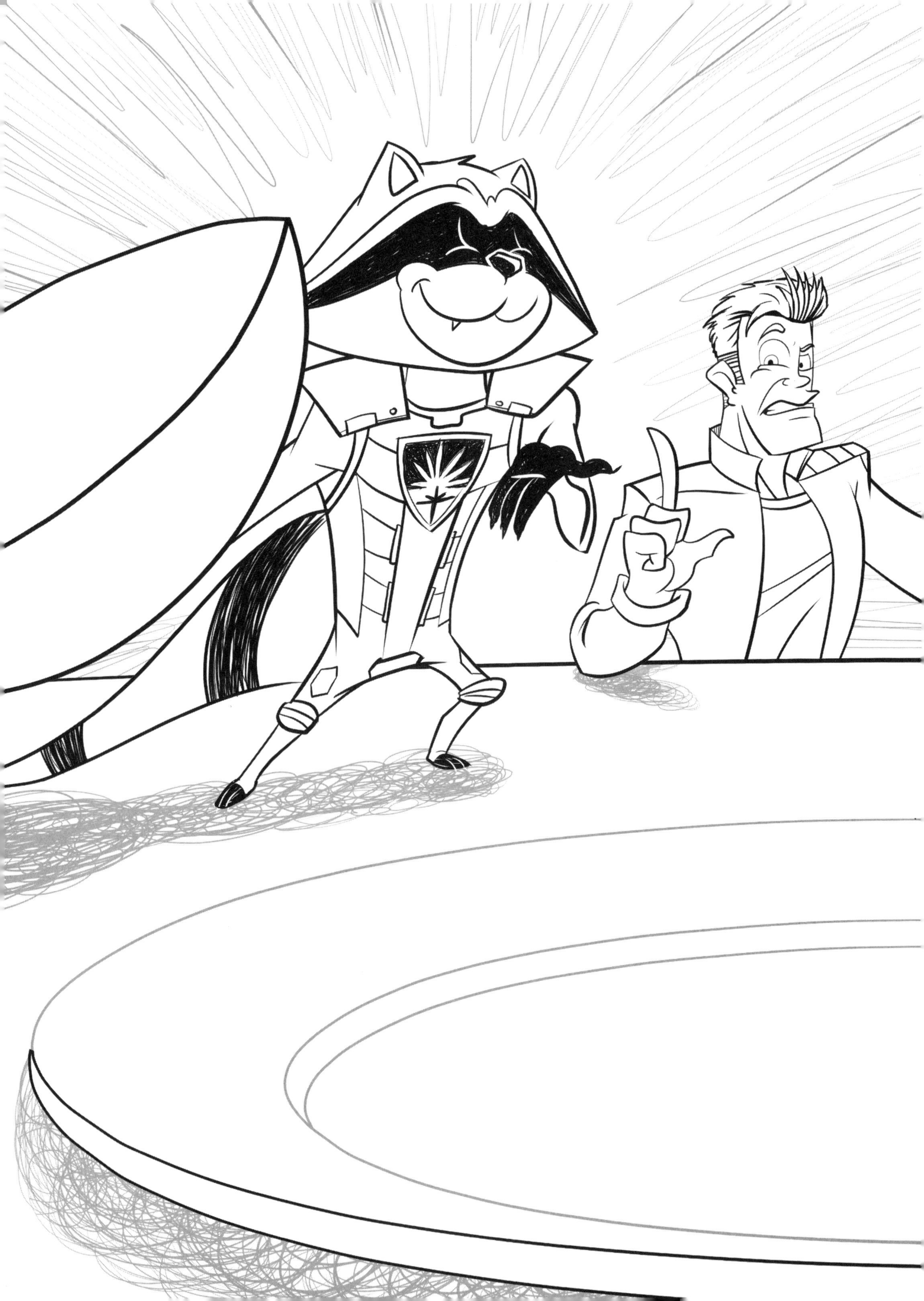

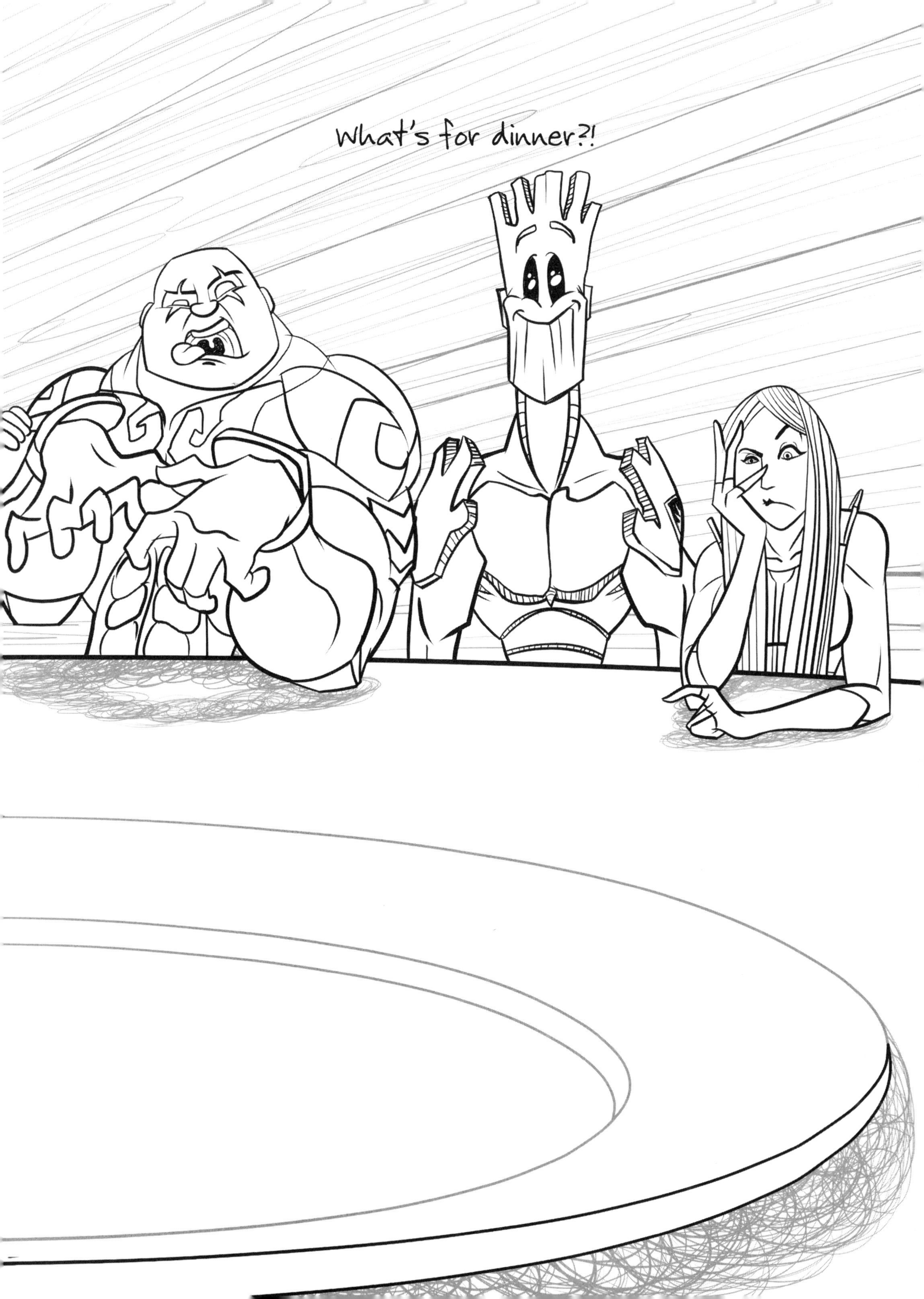
What's for dinner?!

As usual, Star-Lord said the wrong thing to the wrong alien warlord, and now Drax has to defend his honor. AGAIN. Draw a big menacing alien.

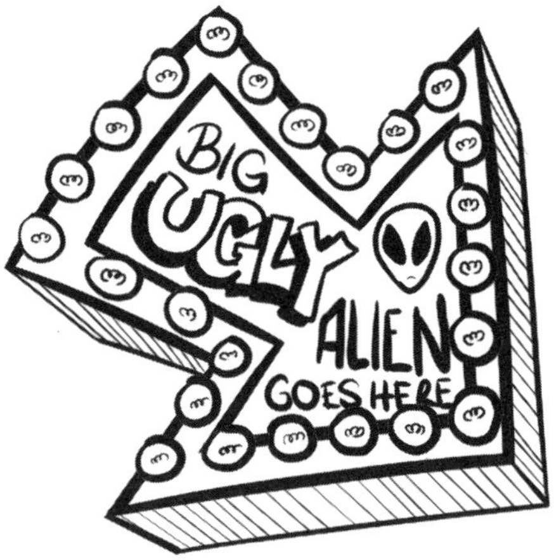
BIG
UGLY
ALIEN
GOES HERE

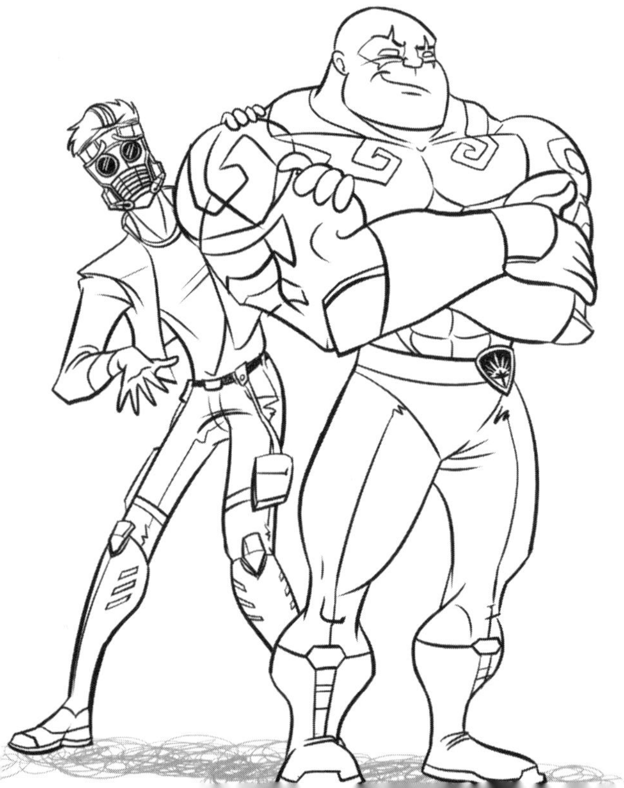

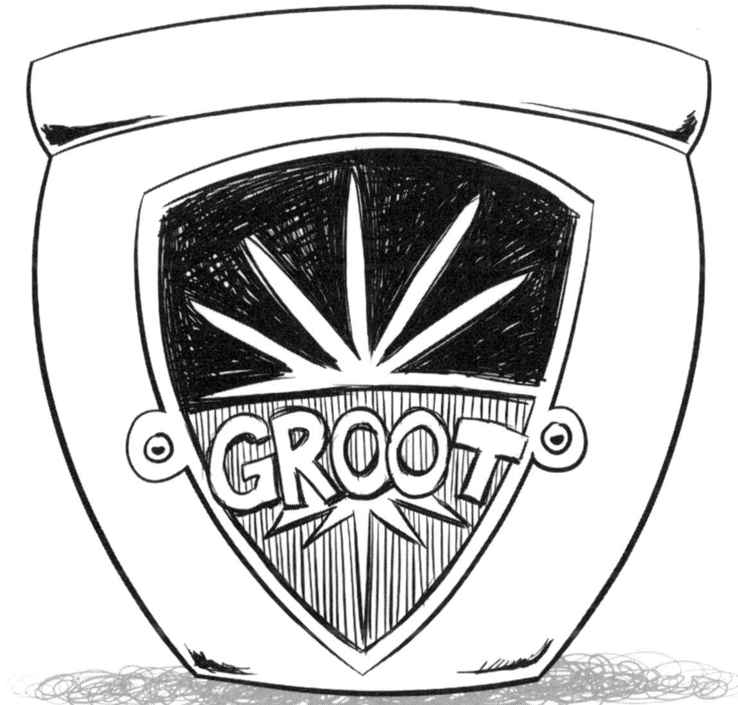
GROOT

Draw your own dancing Groot.
You know you want to!

It looks like Rocket found the Guardians a rental spaceship, but it's a total hunk of garbage.

Draw the junkiest-looking spaceship you've ever seen in your entire life.

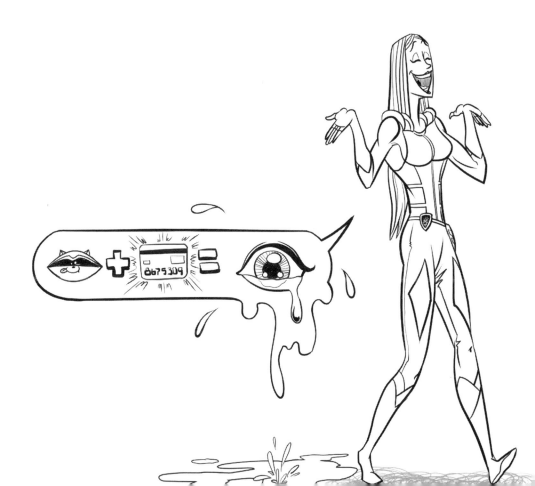

Nebula is way too angry.
Give her a fresh new hairstyle
that will cheer her up for sure.

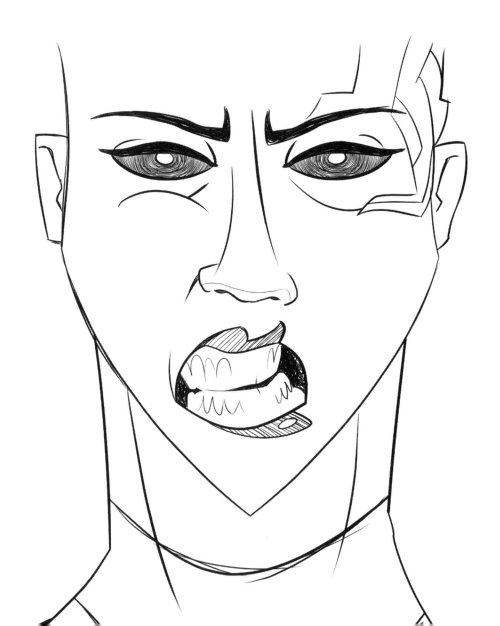

Star-Lord really loves looking at himself.
No surprises there, huh?
Draw his mirror image.

Gamora doodles her thoughts.
It helps her to relax.
What's on her mind today?

Fill this page with GROOTS!
You can draw small Groots and GIANT Groots.
LOTS AND LOTS OF GROOTS!

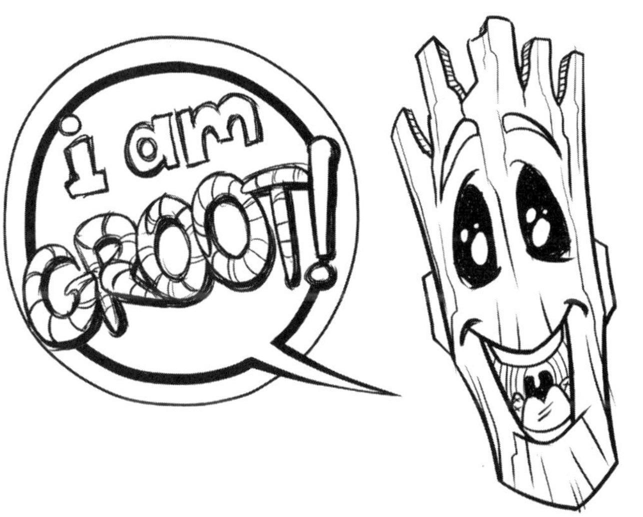
i am GROOT!

The Guardians of the Galaxy are headless!
Draw them each a brand-new noggin.

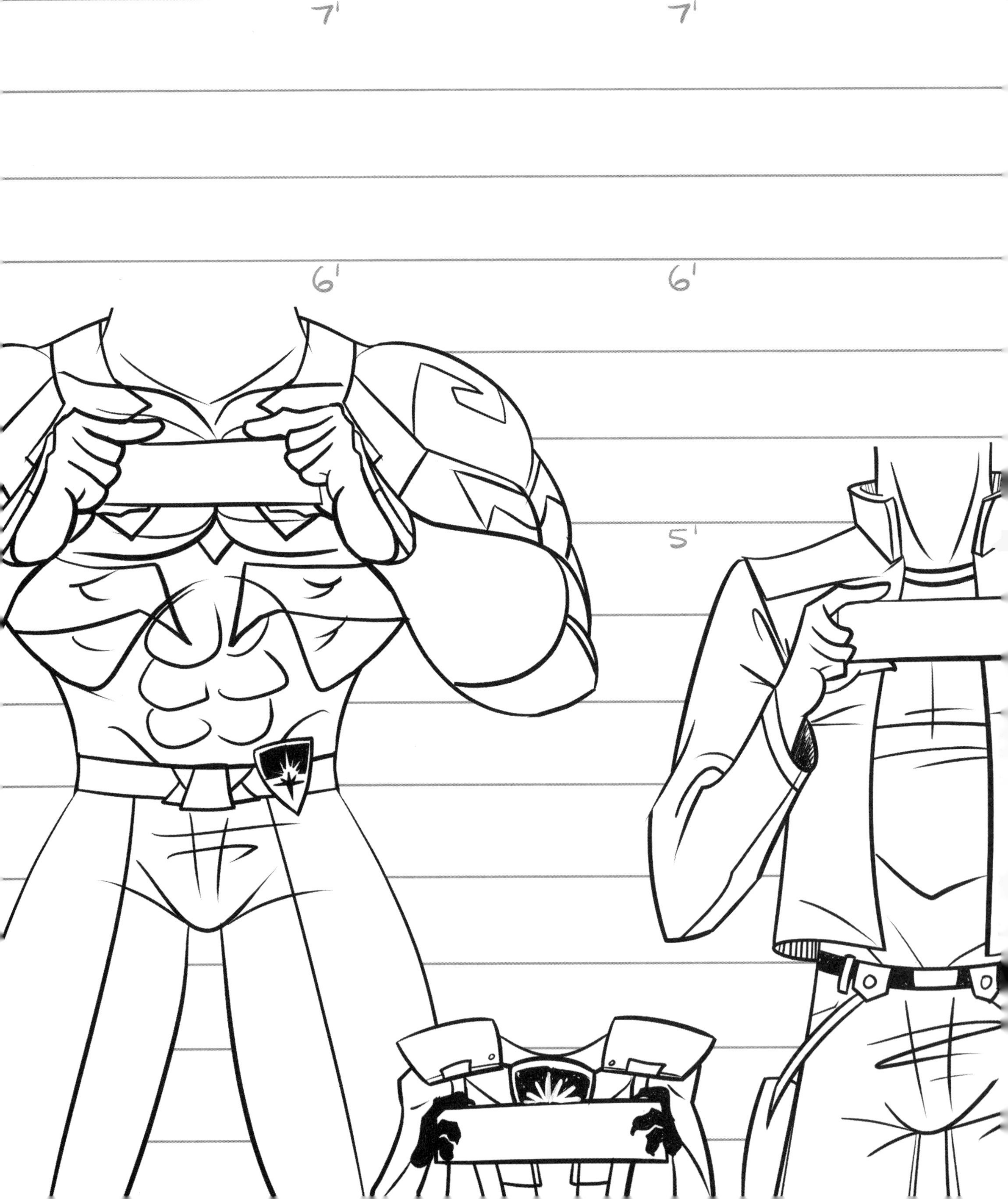
7'
7'
6'
6'
5'

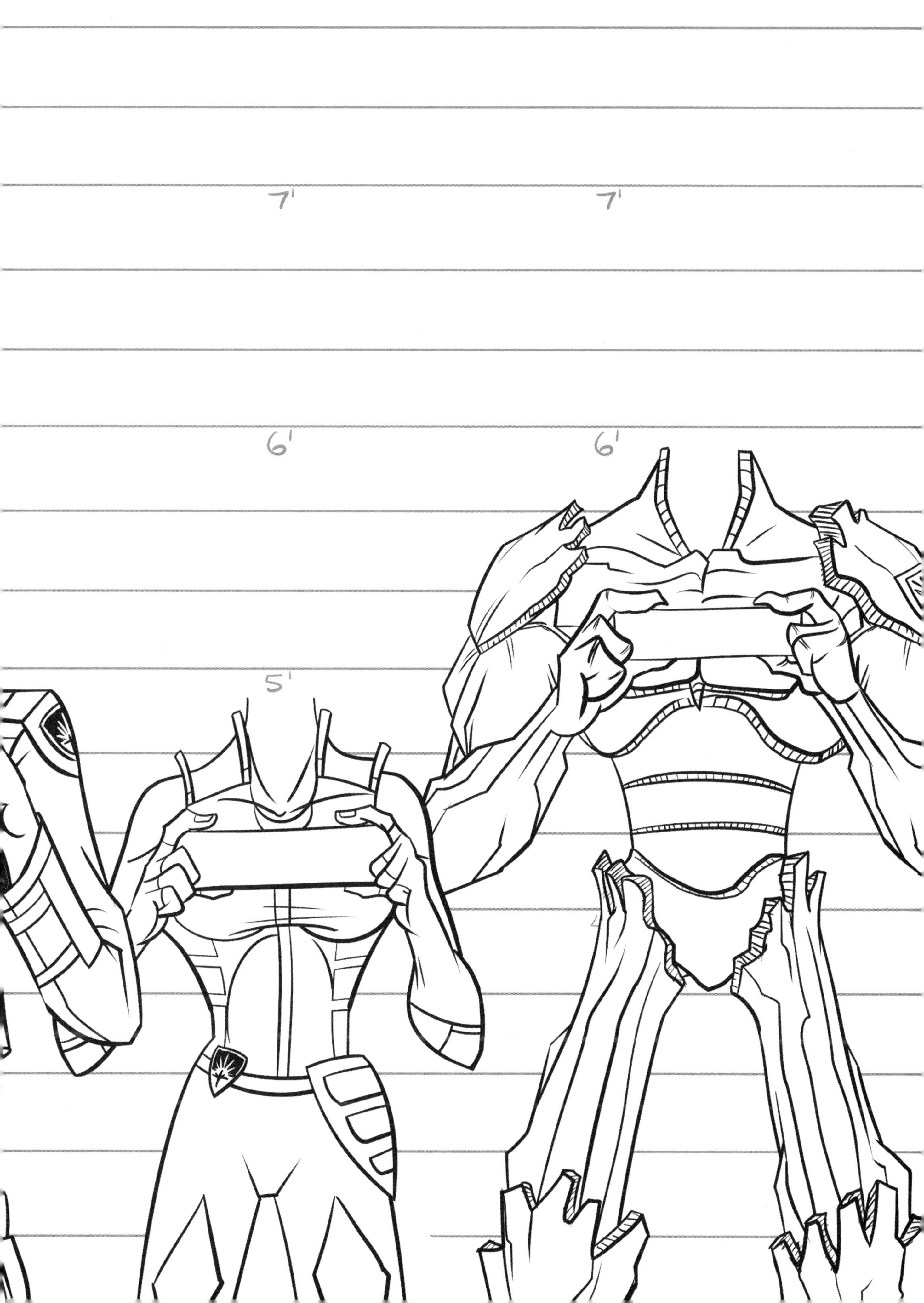
7'
7'
6'
6'
5'

It's raining BUGS!
Draw tons of creepy-crawlies falling
from the sky.

Whose scary eyes are these?!?!
Draw a menacing face and head
around them.

 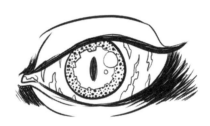

Someone stole the entire galaxy!
How does this keep happening?

Draw lots and lots of new planets.
Make 'em BIG and make 'em small.
Don't forget to top it all off with
a nice warm SUN.

Drax wishes he had hair so he could
rock the craziest hairstyle in the universe.
Draw him some and make his dream come true.

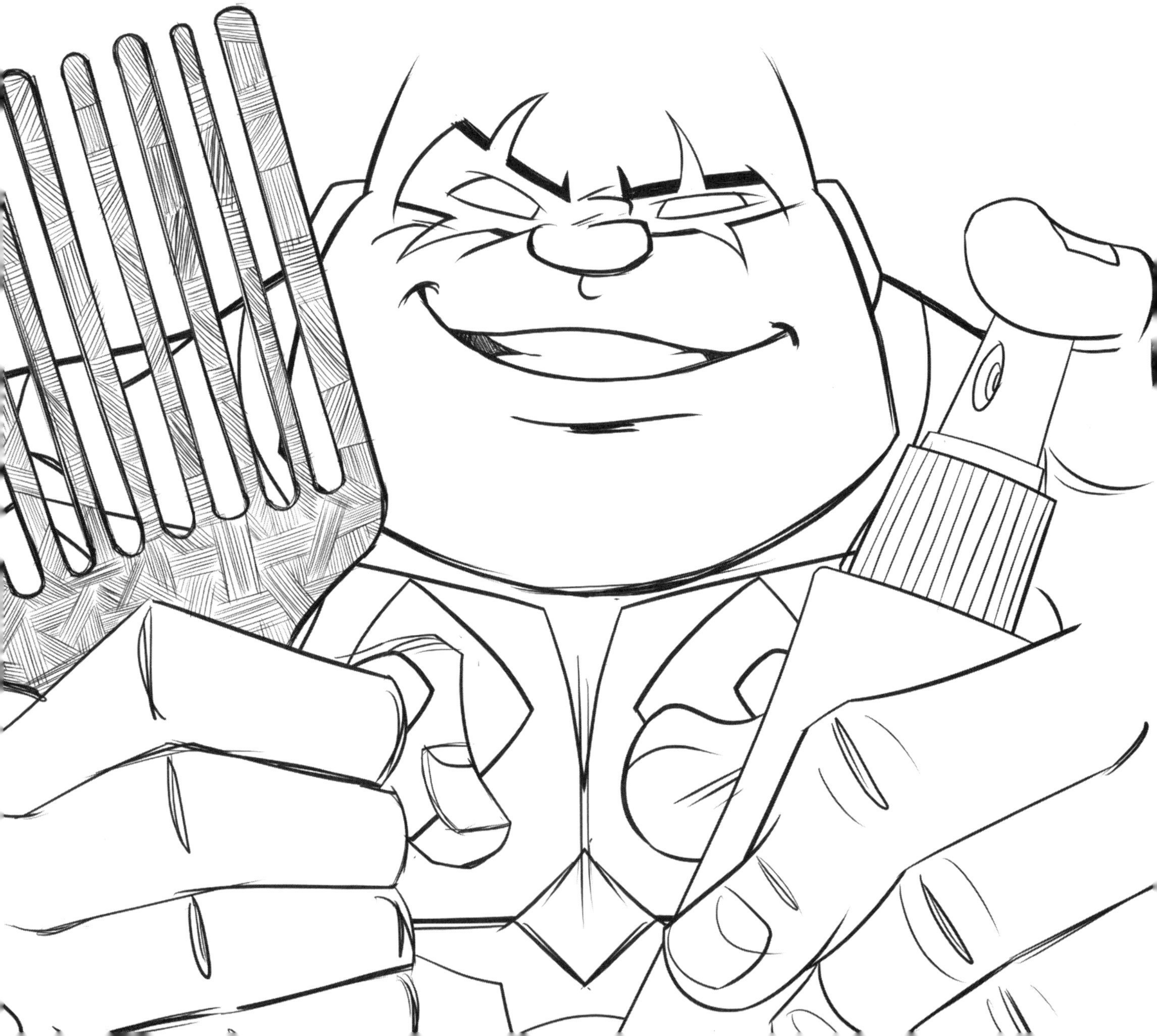

Rocket is desperate for a snack.
What should he have?

Draw a lot of gross options
for him to choose from.

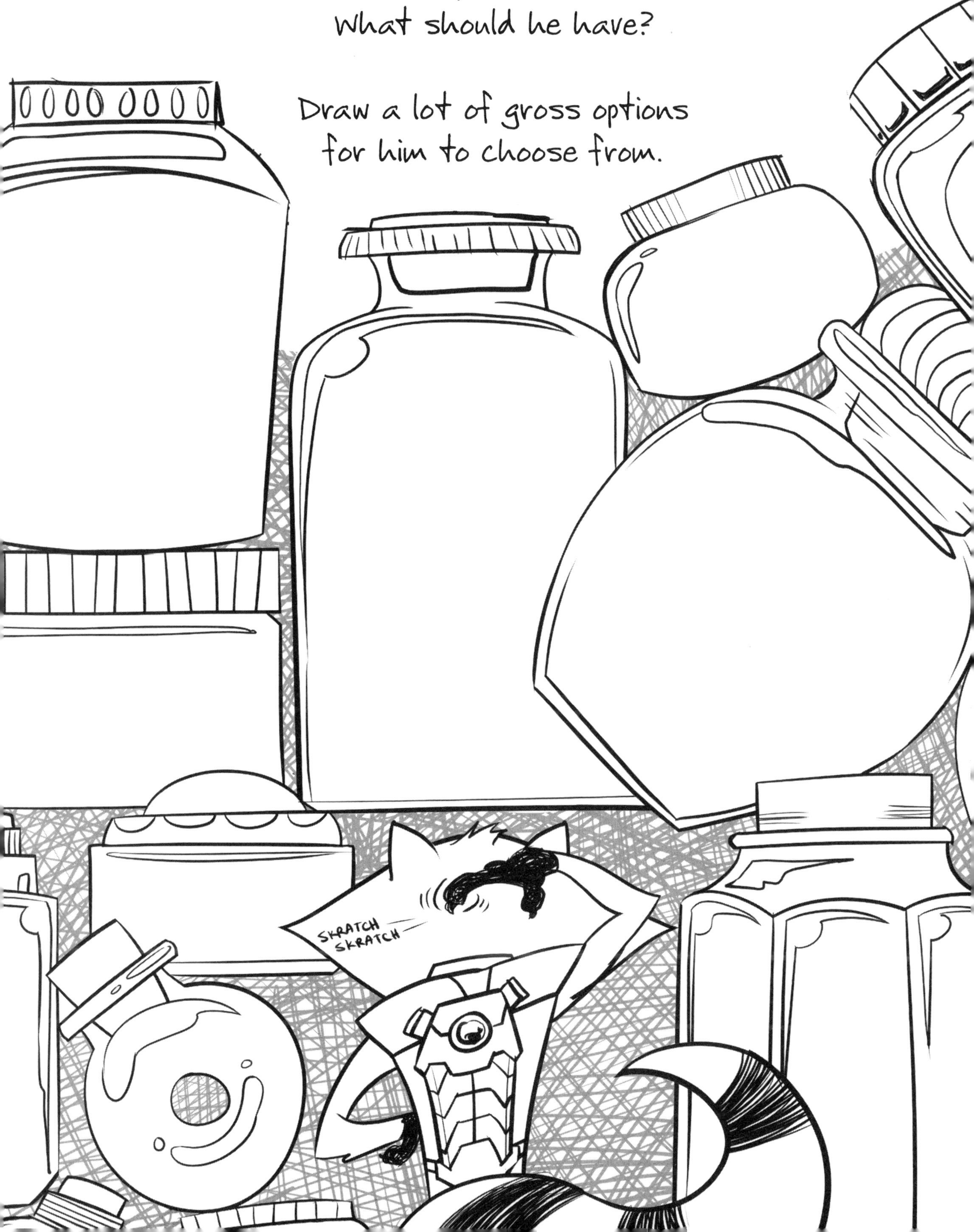
SKRATCH
SKRATCH

Star-Lord had his own face airbrushed on the back of his jacket, but it looks a little weird. Why is that? Draw it and find out!

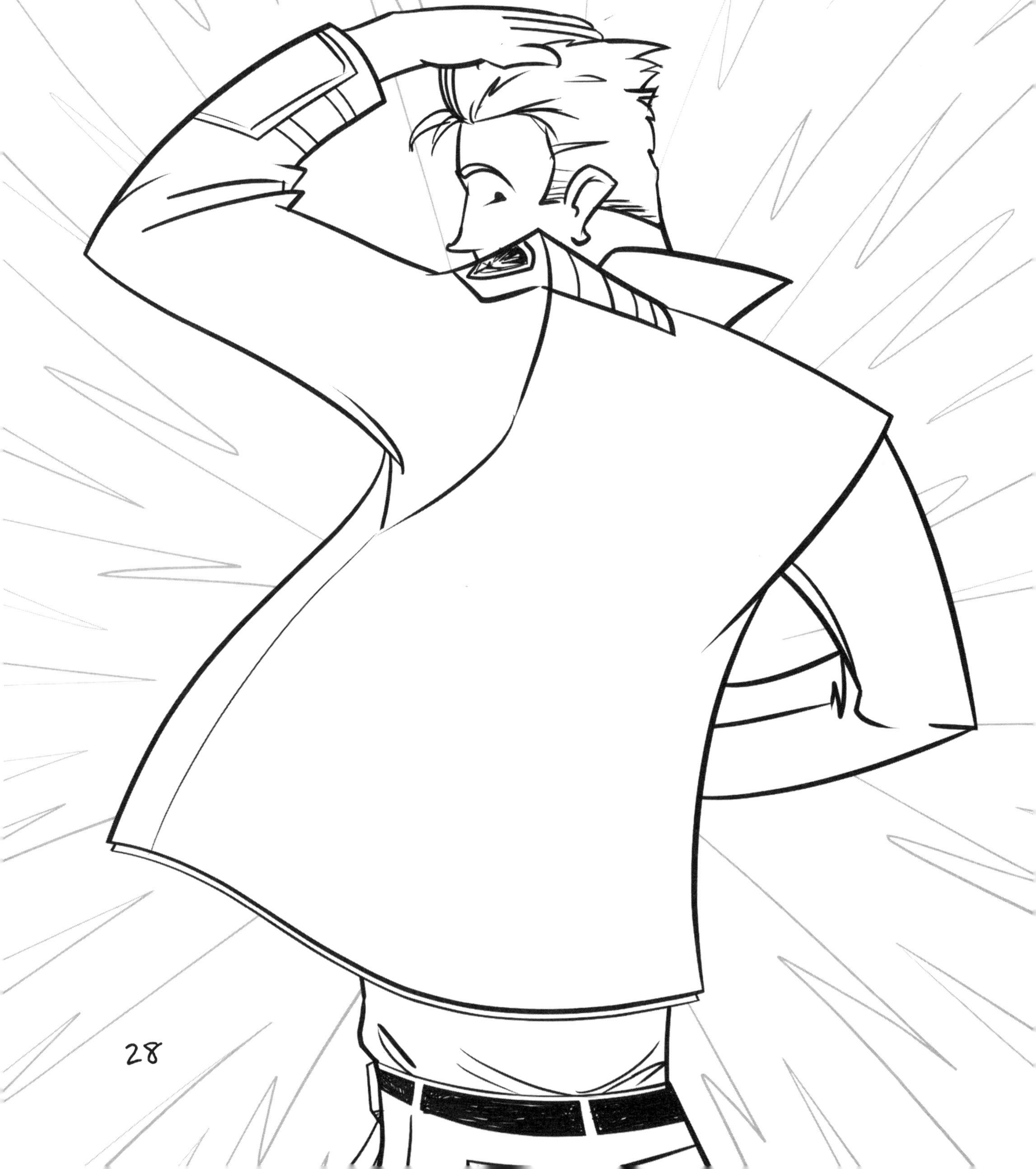

Turn this circle into
something dangerous and weird.
The drawing of tentacles is encouraged!

A battalion of Chitauri soldiers are chasing after
Gamora. Draw LOTS of them!
(Don't worry, she can handle it.)

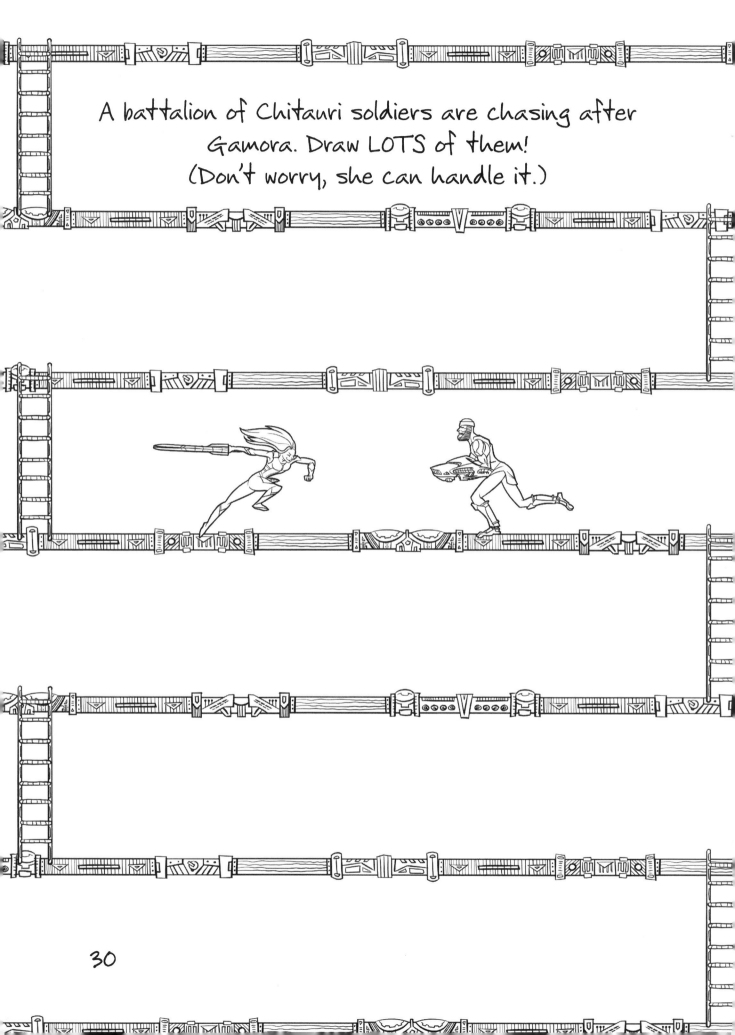

Groot is so angry that steam
is coming out of his ears.
Draw his ferocious frowny face.

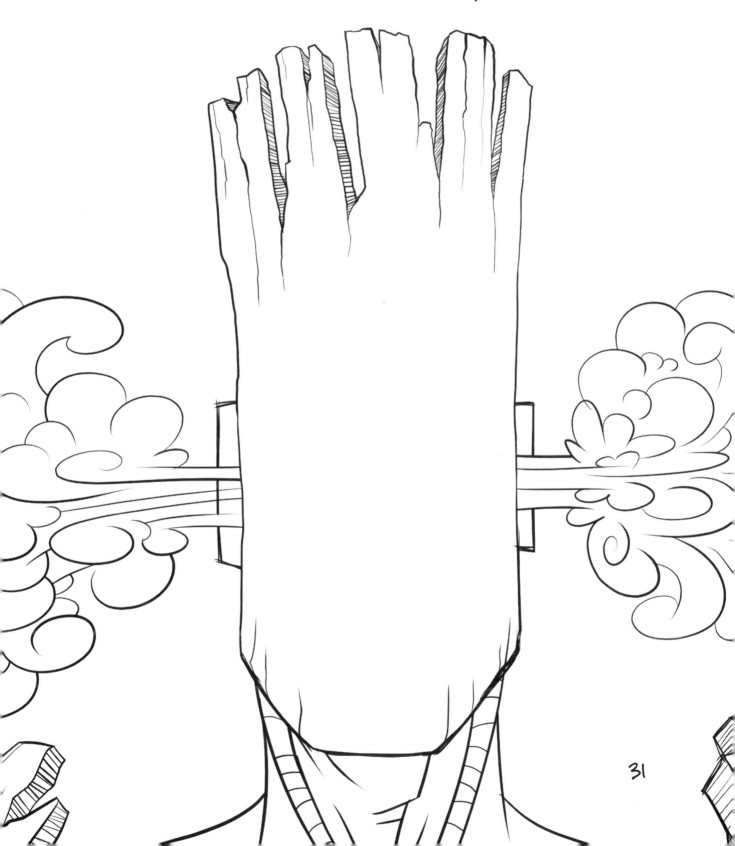

31

Star-Lord and Rocket spray-painted graffiti all over Nebula's ship, and she's NOT happy about it.

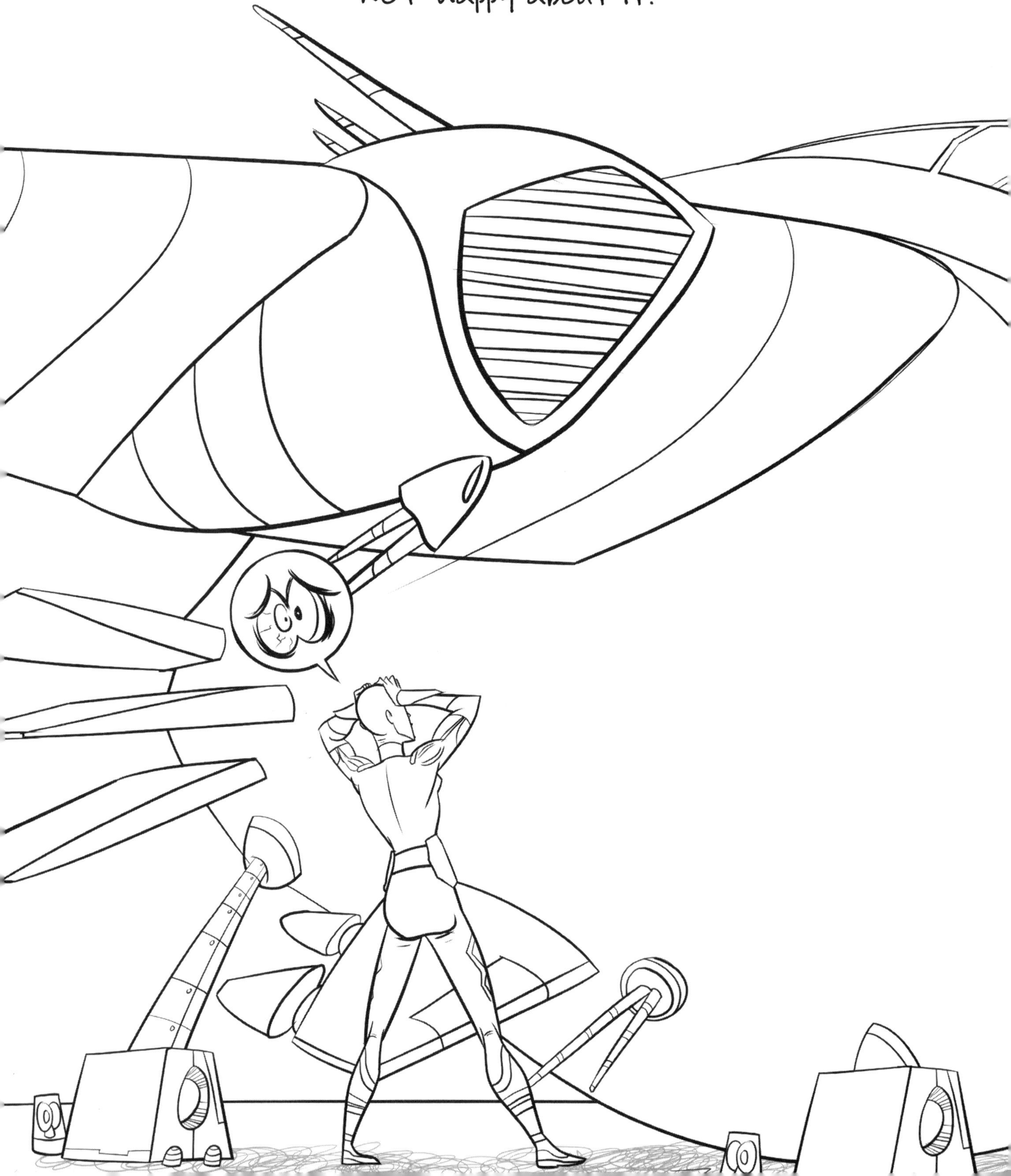

Draw some graffiti that would make Nebula steaming mad.

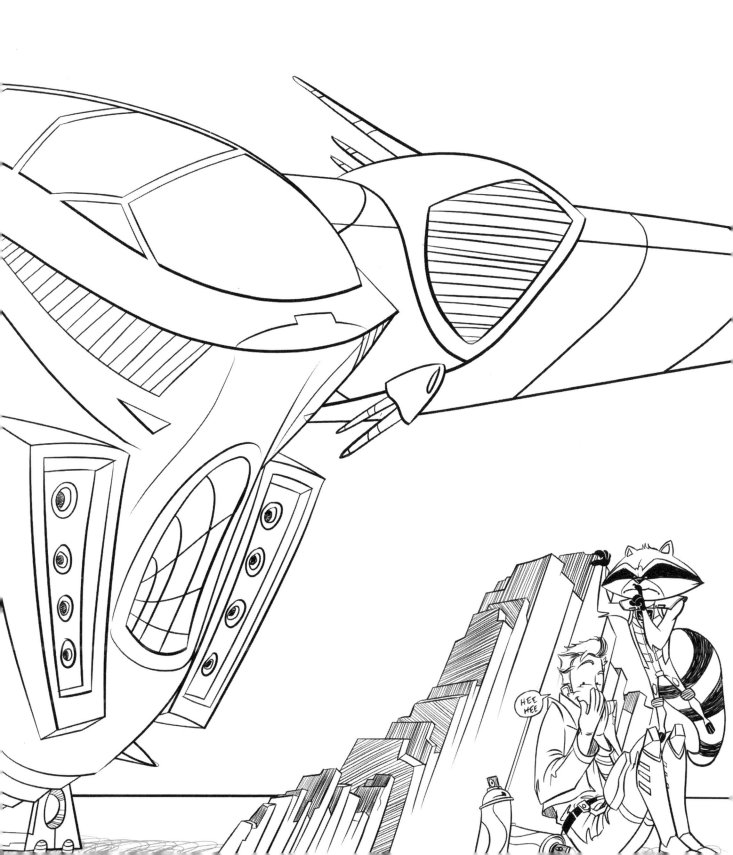

Strange cosmic energies turned Drax and Gamora
into little bitty baby versions of themselves.
Draw them looking as cute as a bug in a rug.

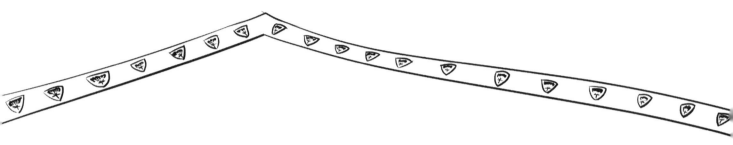

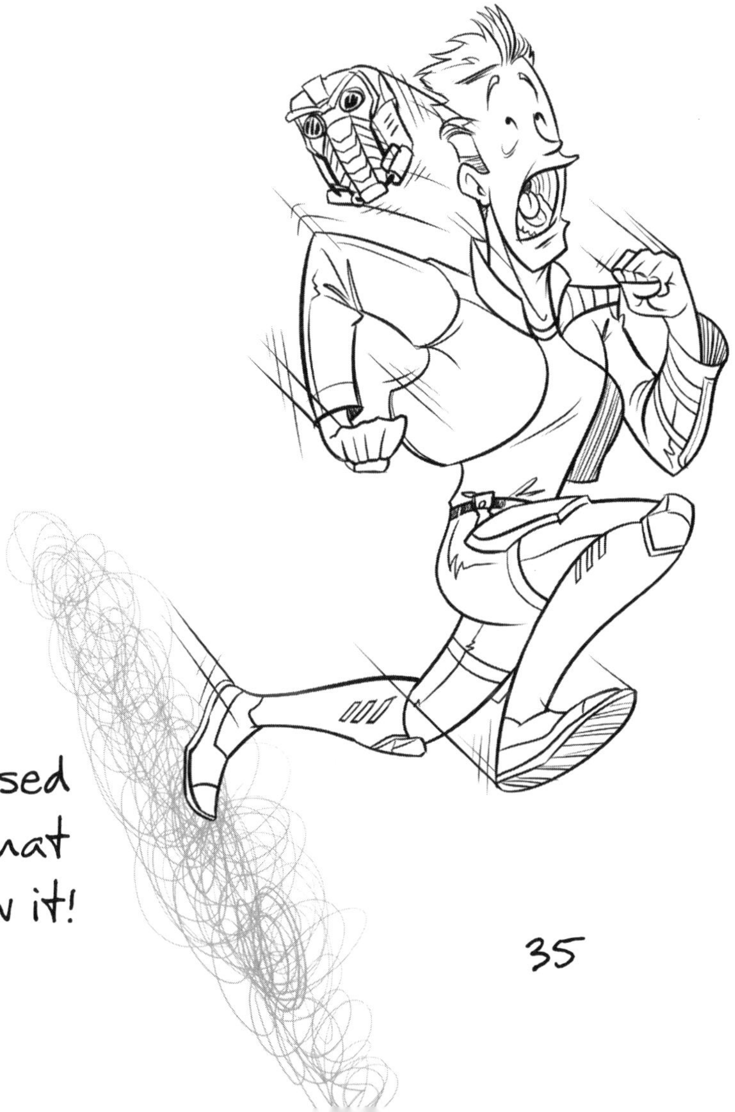

Star-Lord is being chased by an alien creature that wants to eat him. Draw it!

What is Gamora holding?

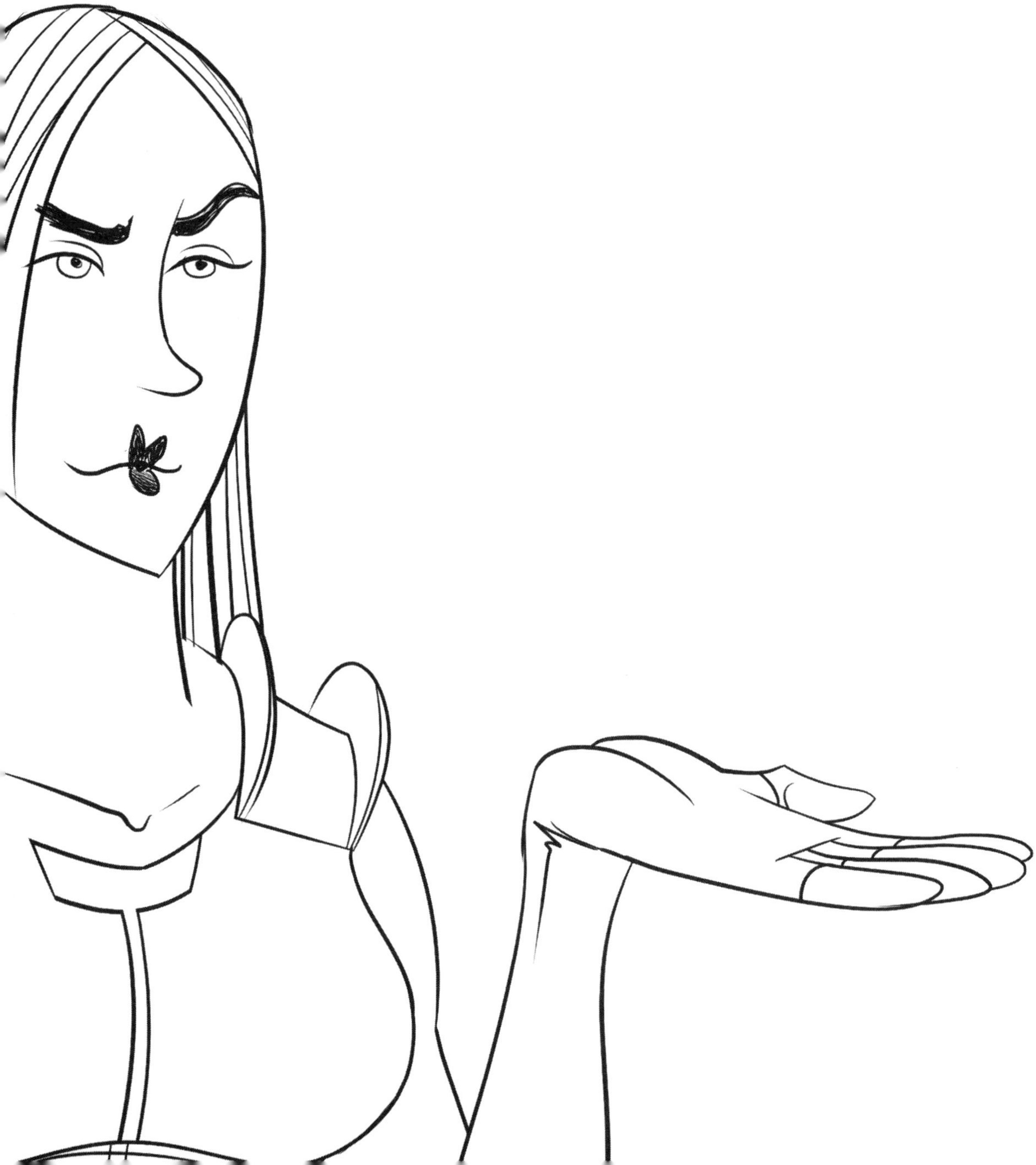

Groot's hair is a giant, leafy bush.
Draw it!

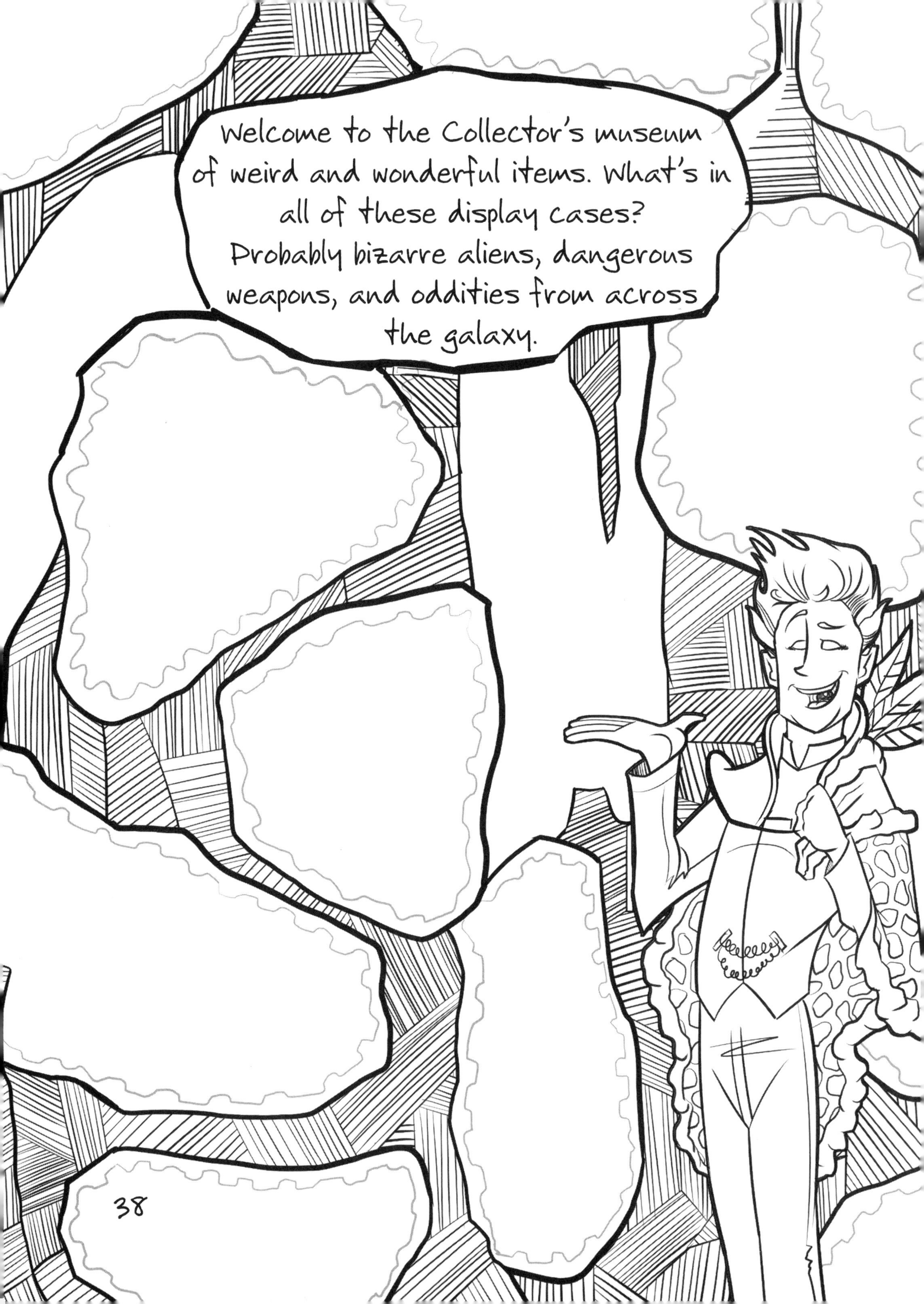
Welcome to the Collector's museum of weird and wonderful items. What's in all of these display cases? Probably bizarre aliens, dangerous weapons, and oddities from across the galaxy.

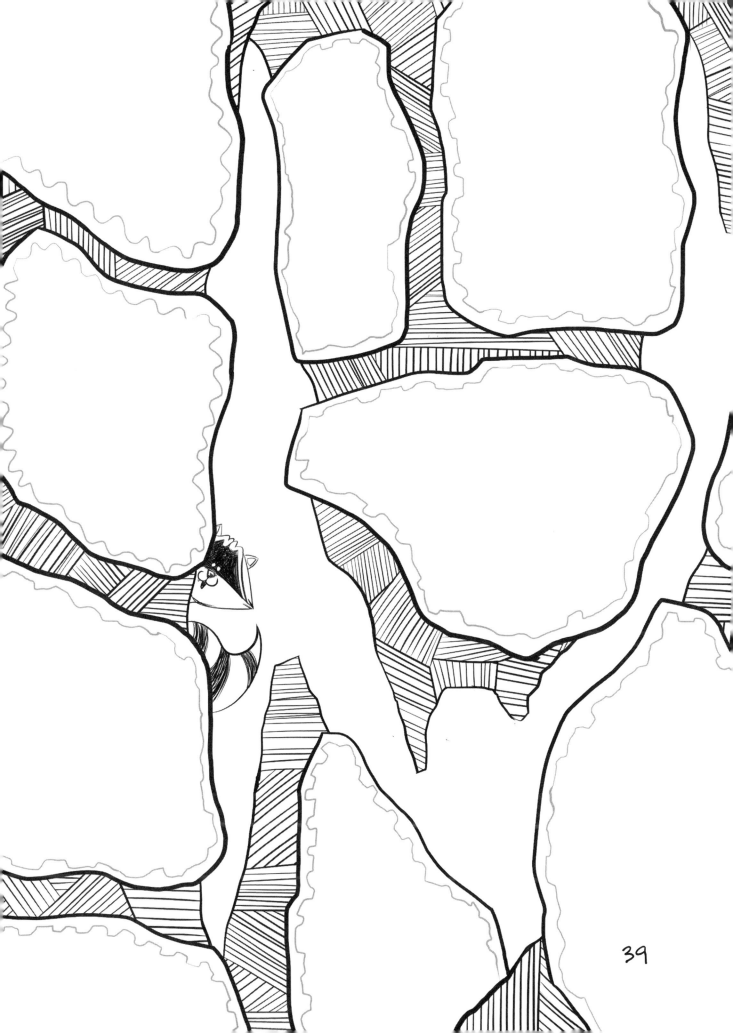

39

It's raining GUNK!
Give the Guardians some super-big (and just plain crazy-looking) hats that will protect their beautiful heads.

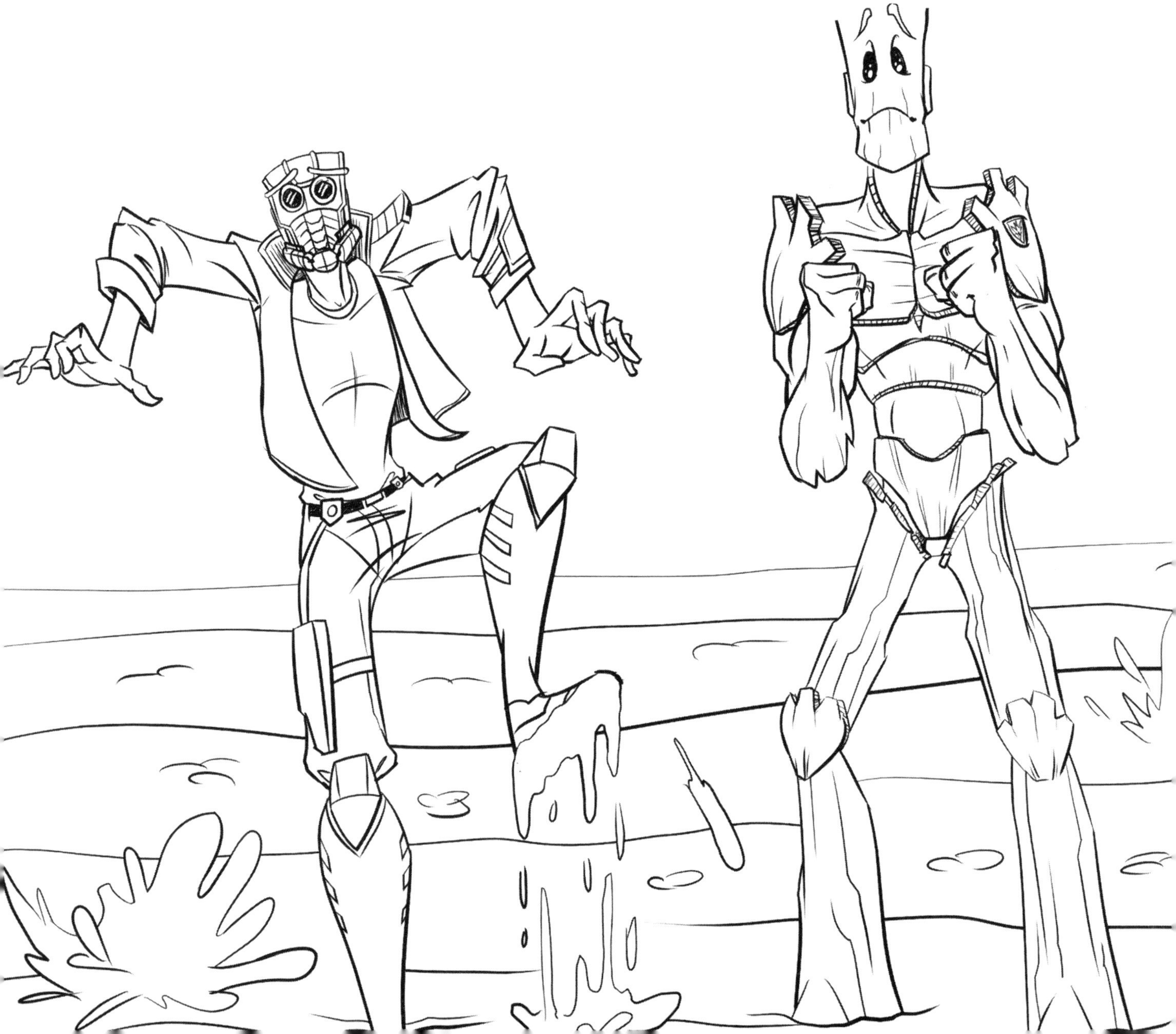

Oh, and draw lots of icky GUNK, too.

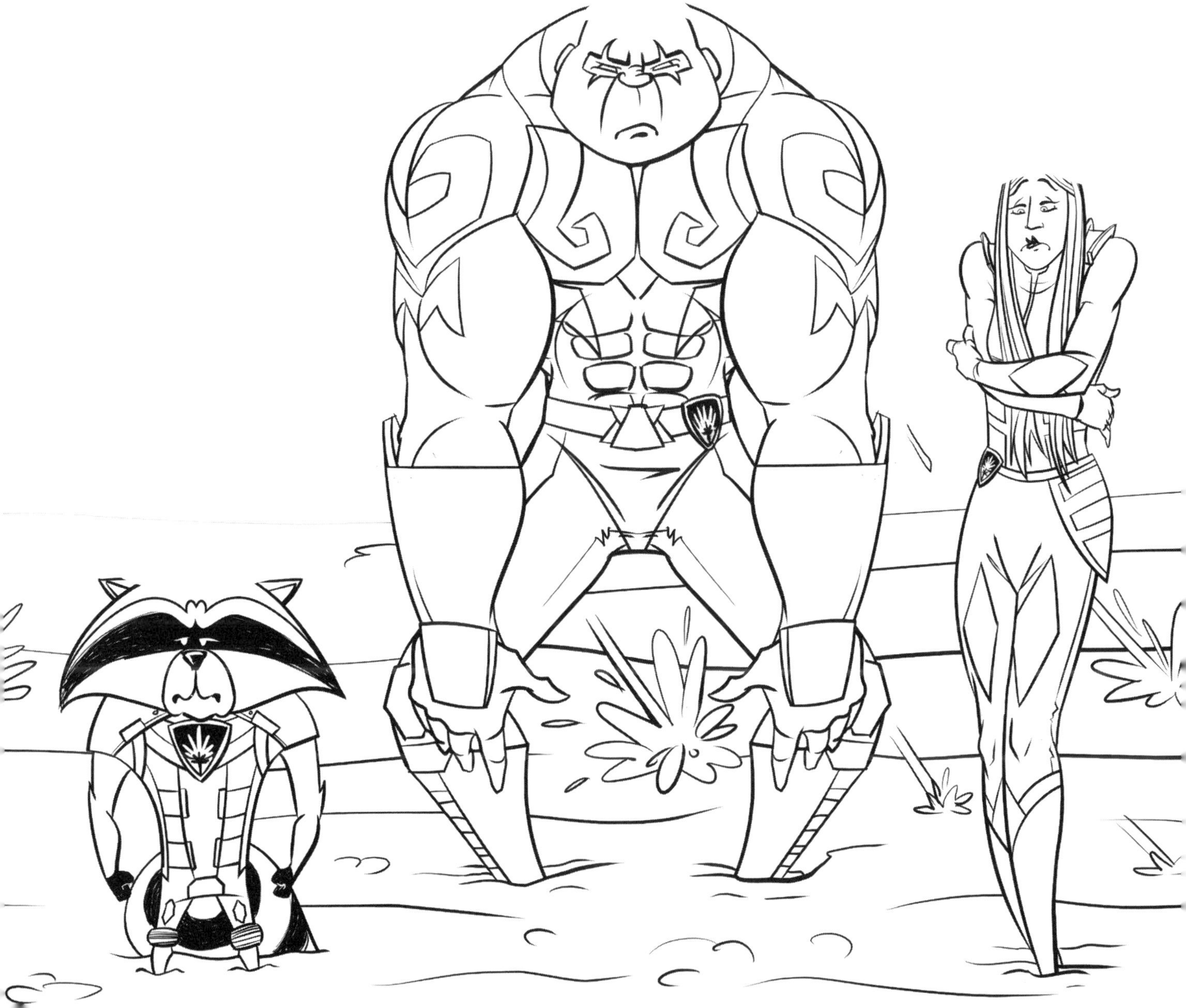

Star-Lord sure is dodging a lot of laser fire.
He must have done something naughty.
Draw lots and lots of colorful lasers that'll help
him learn a lesson.

Sure is hot and humid out, huh?
Now Rocket's luxurious mane is extra fluffy.
Draw his new hairdo and make it extra poofy.

Giant beasts are chasing
the Guardians across the desert.
Draw them!

DRAW HERE!

AND HERE!...

...MIGHT AS WELL FILL THE PAGE.

Draw Gamora's head on Star-Lord's body.
C'mon! It'll be fun.

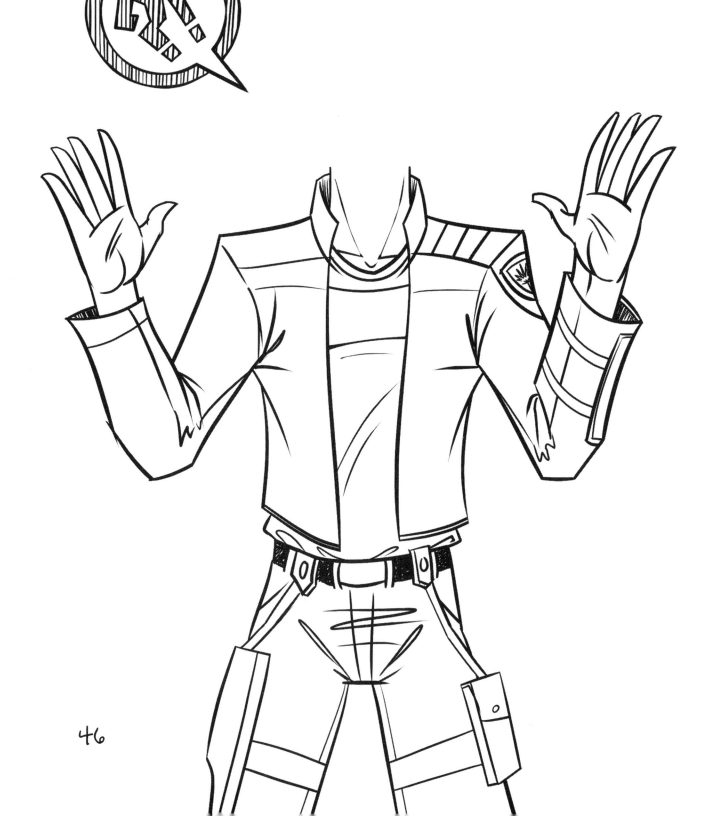

Design a new sword for Gamora!
Make extra sure it's good at deflecting lasers.

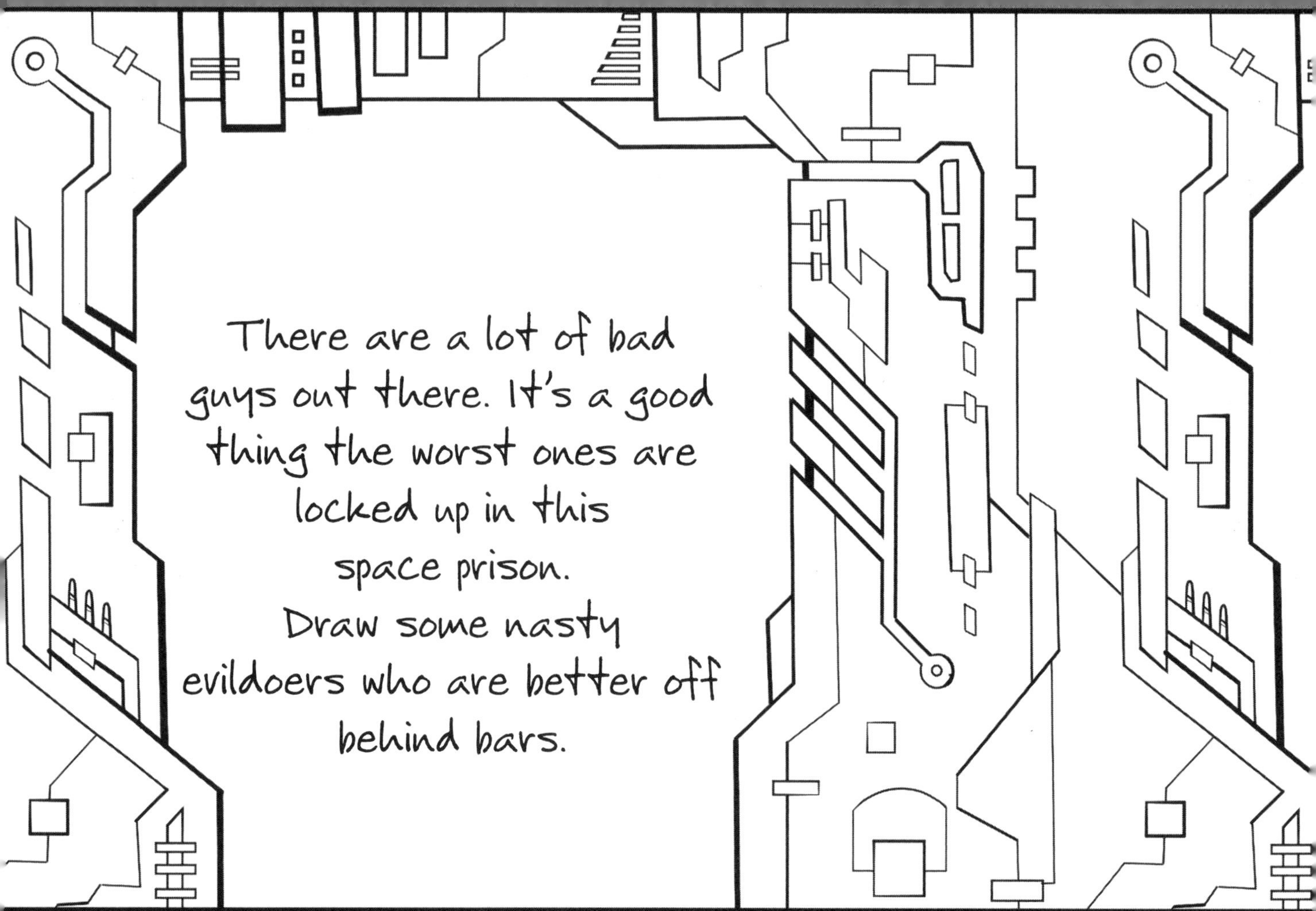

There are a lot of bad guys out there. It's a good thing the worst ones are locked up in this space prison.
Draw some nasty evildoers who are better off behind bars.

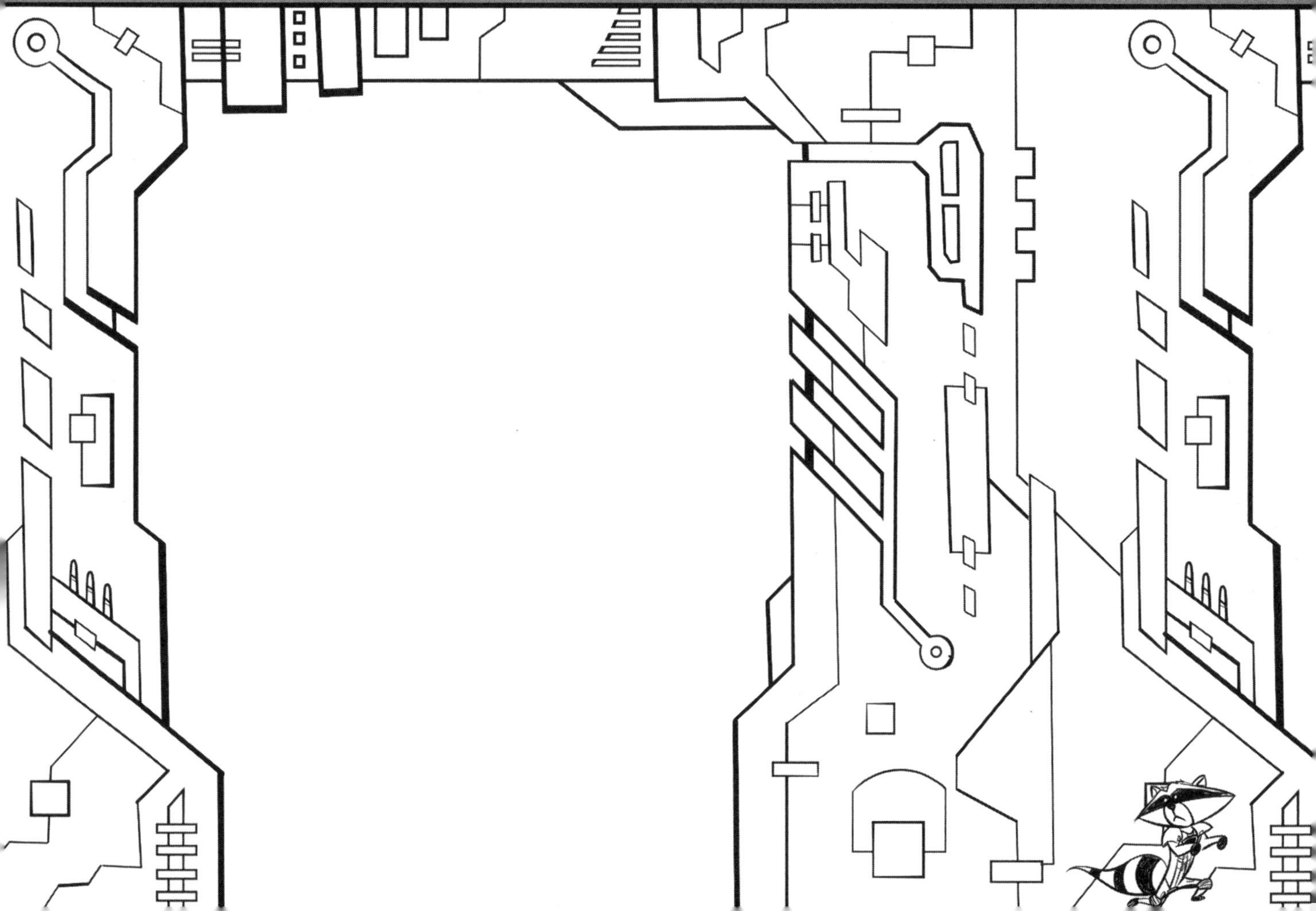

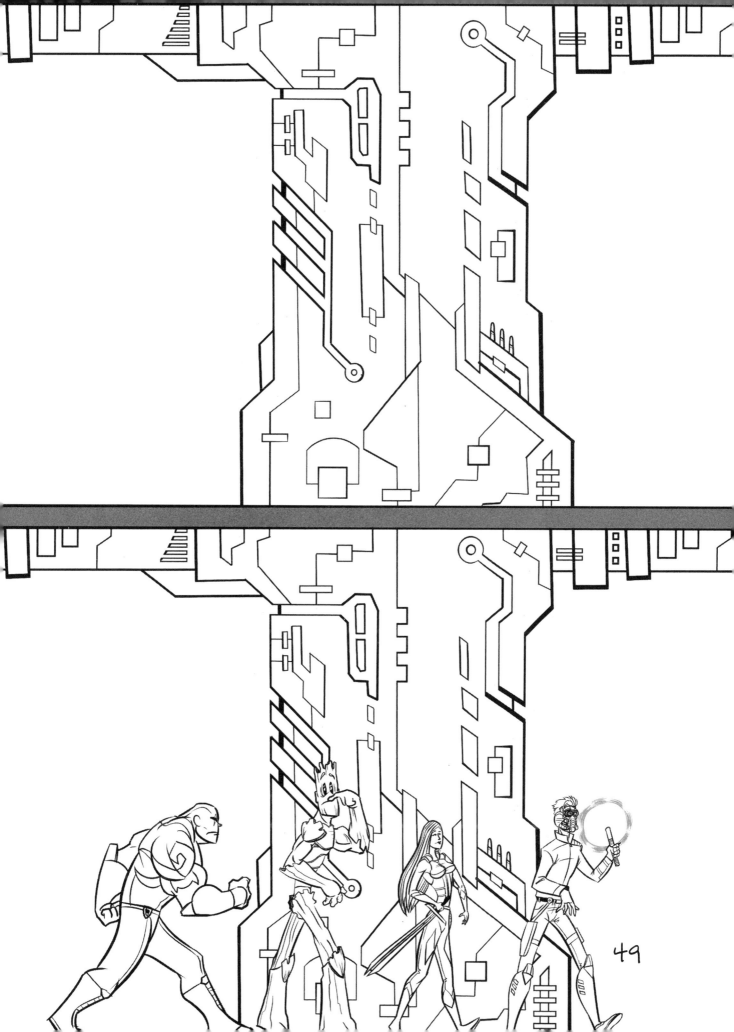

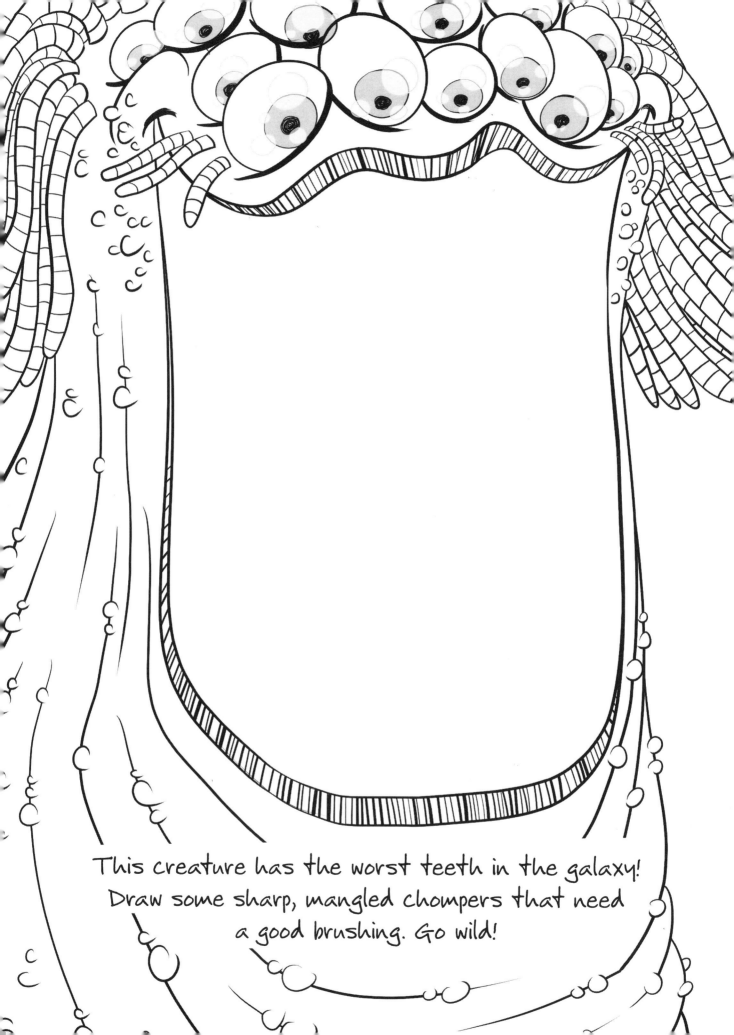

This creature has the worst teeth in the galaxy!
Draw some sharp, mangled chompers that need
a good brushing. Go wild!

Thanos used the power of the Infinity Stones to shrink the Guardians of the Galaxy down and put them in a snow globe.
What are they doing in there?!

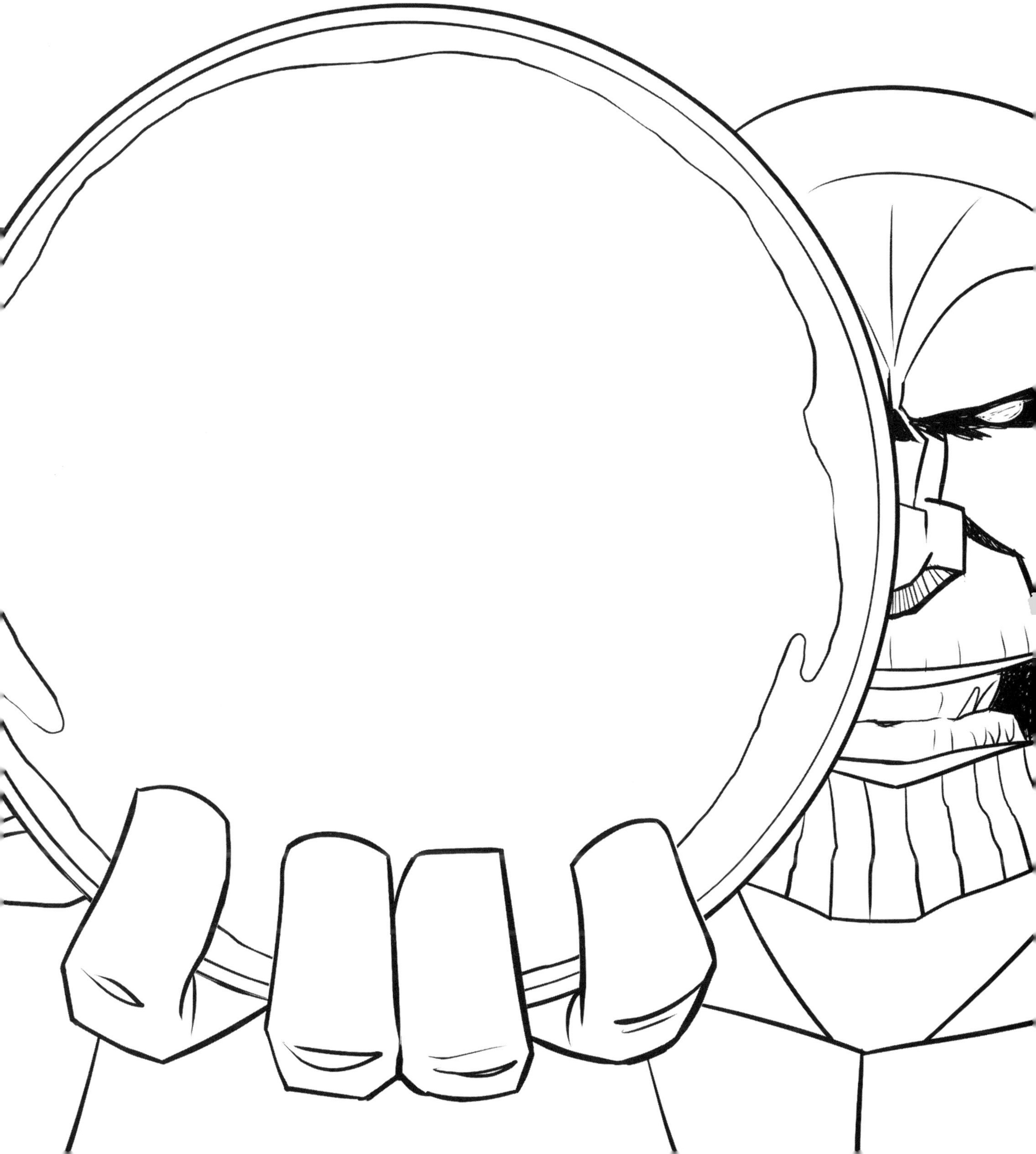

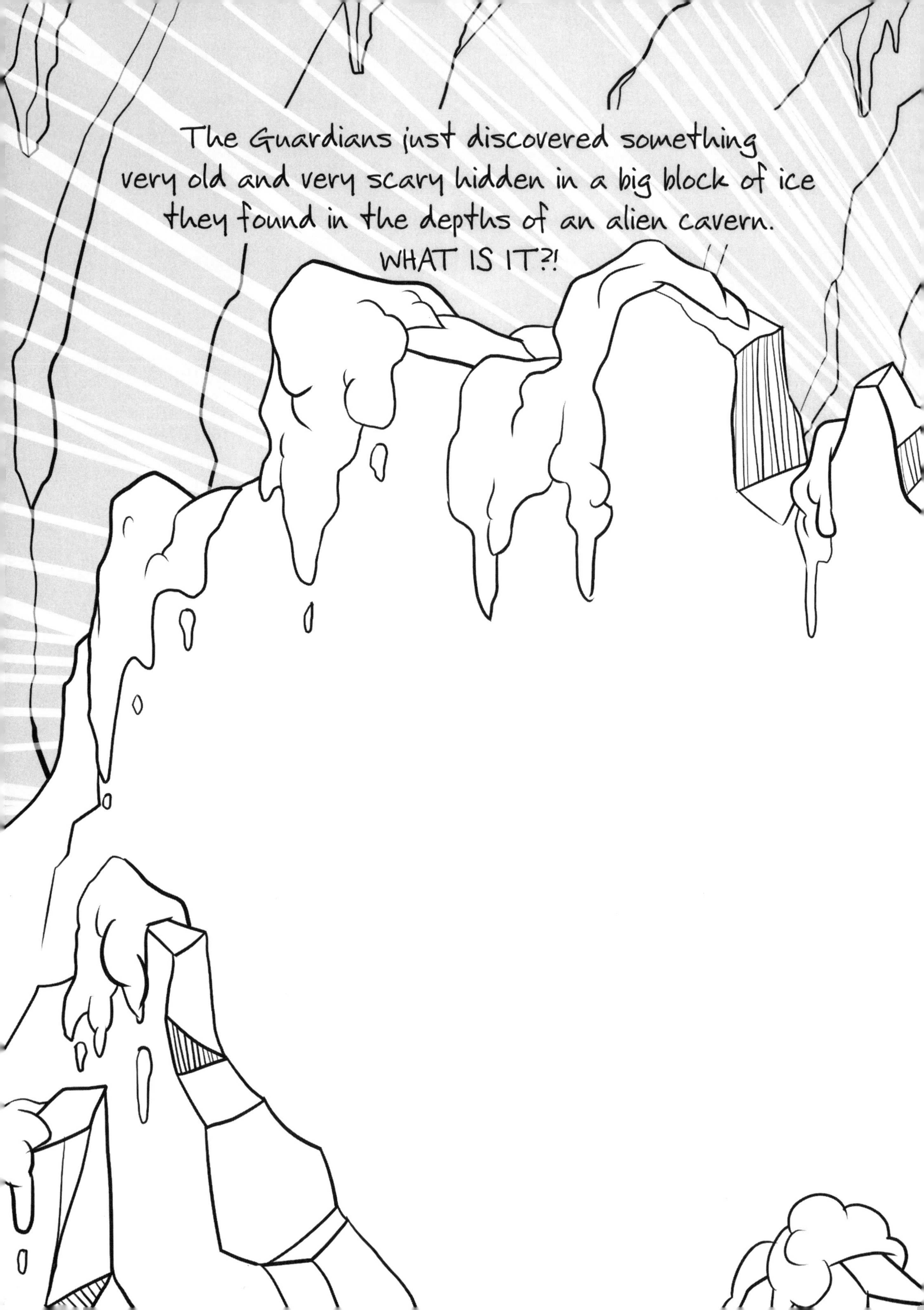
The Guardians just discovered something very old and very scary hidden in a big block of ice they found in the depths of an alien cavern.
WHAT IS IT?!

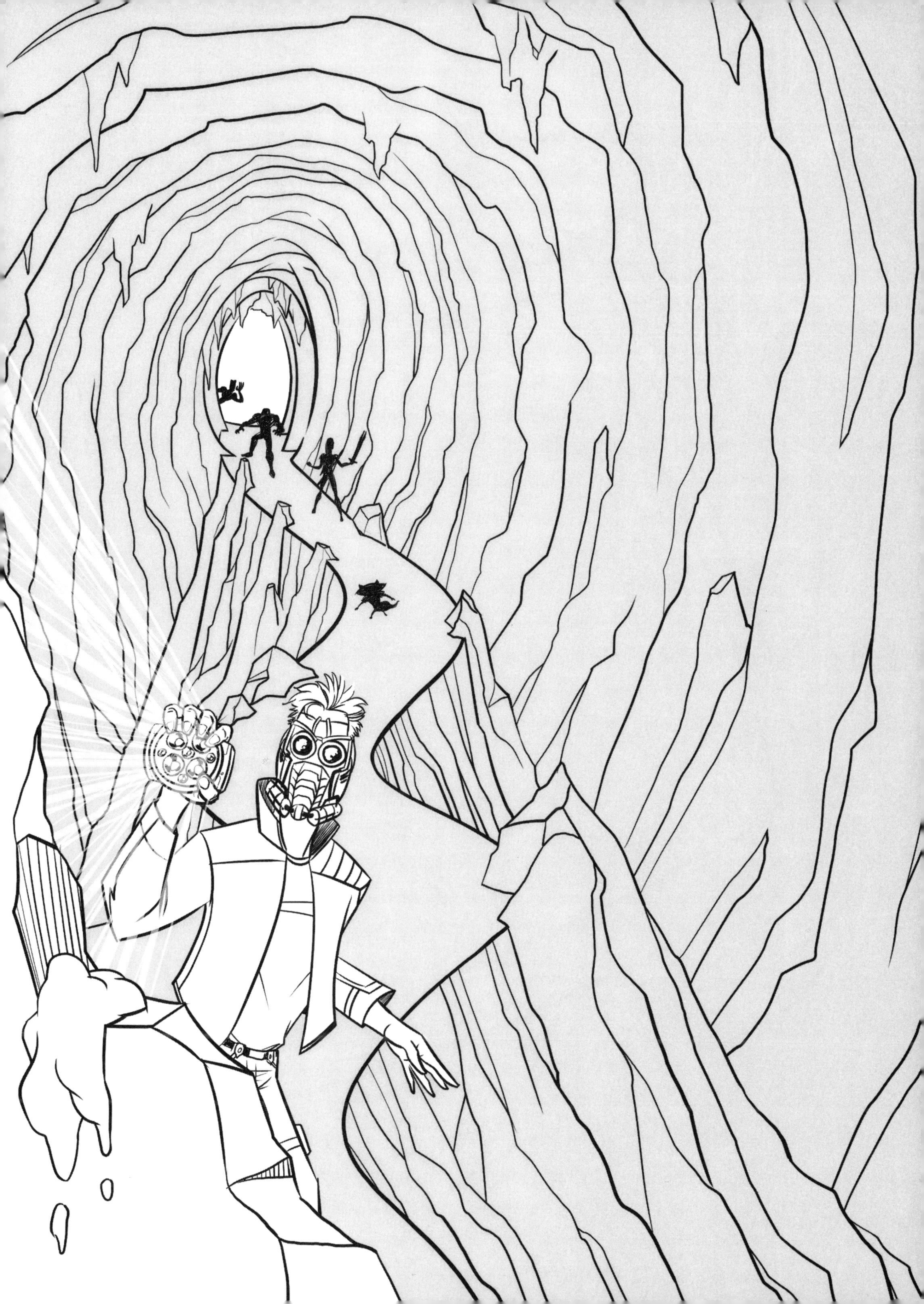

Who's in Drax's favorite photograph?

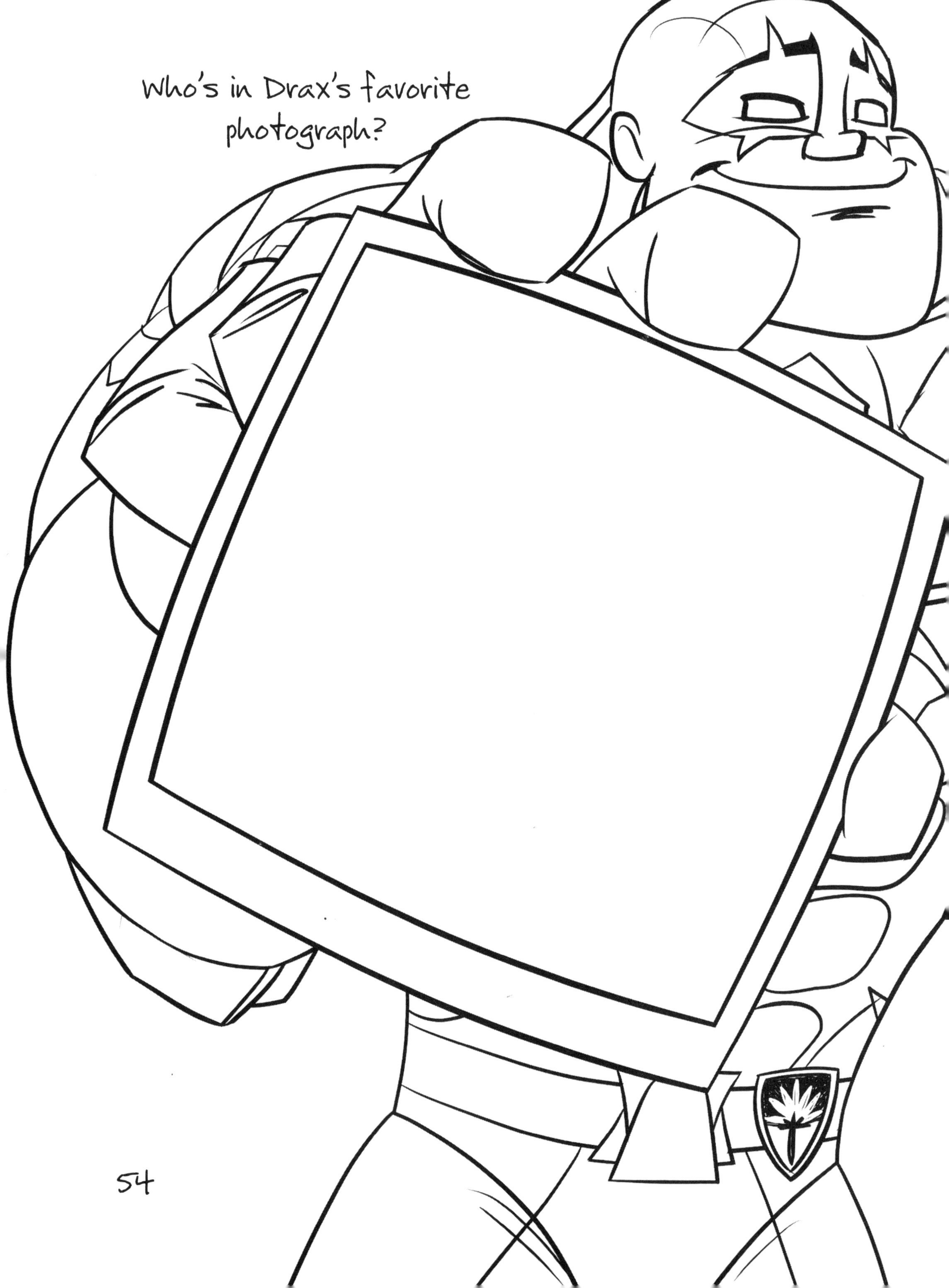

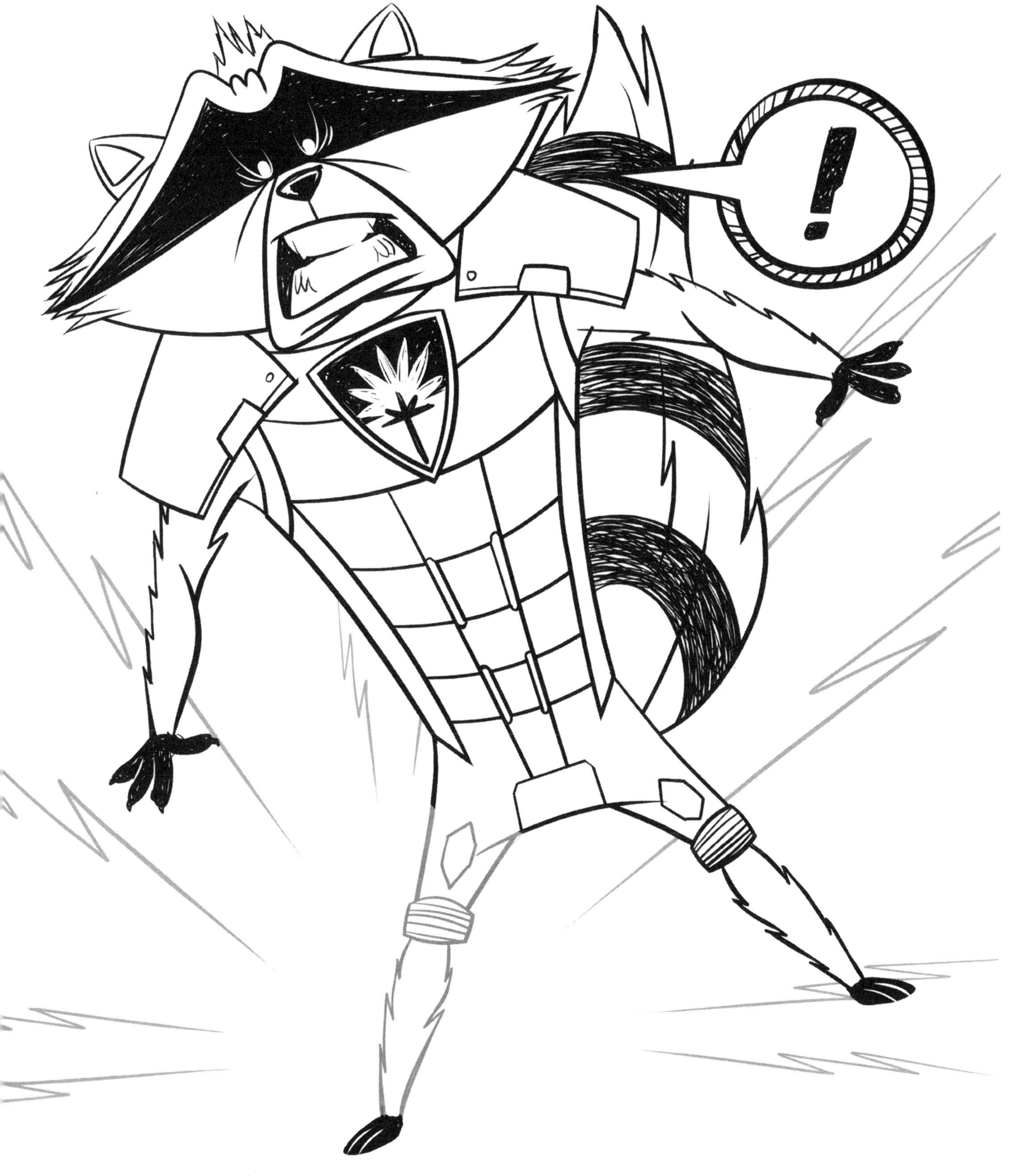
!

Something is crawling up Rocket's leg!
Get it off! GET IT OFF!

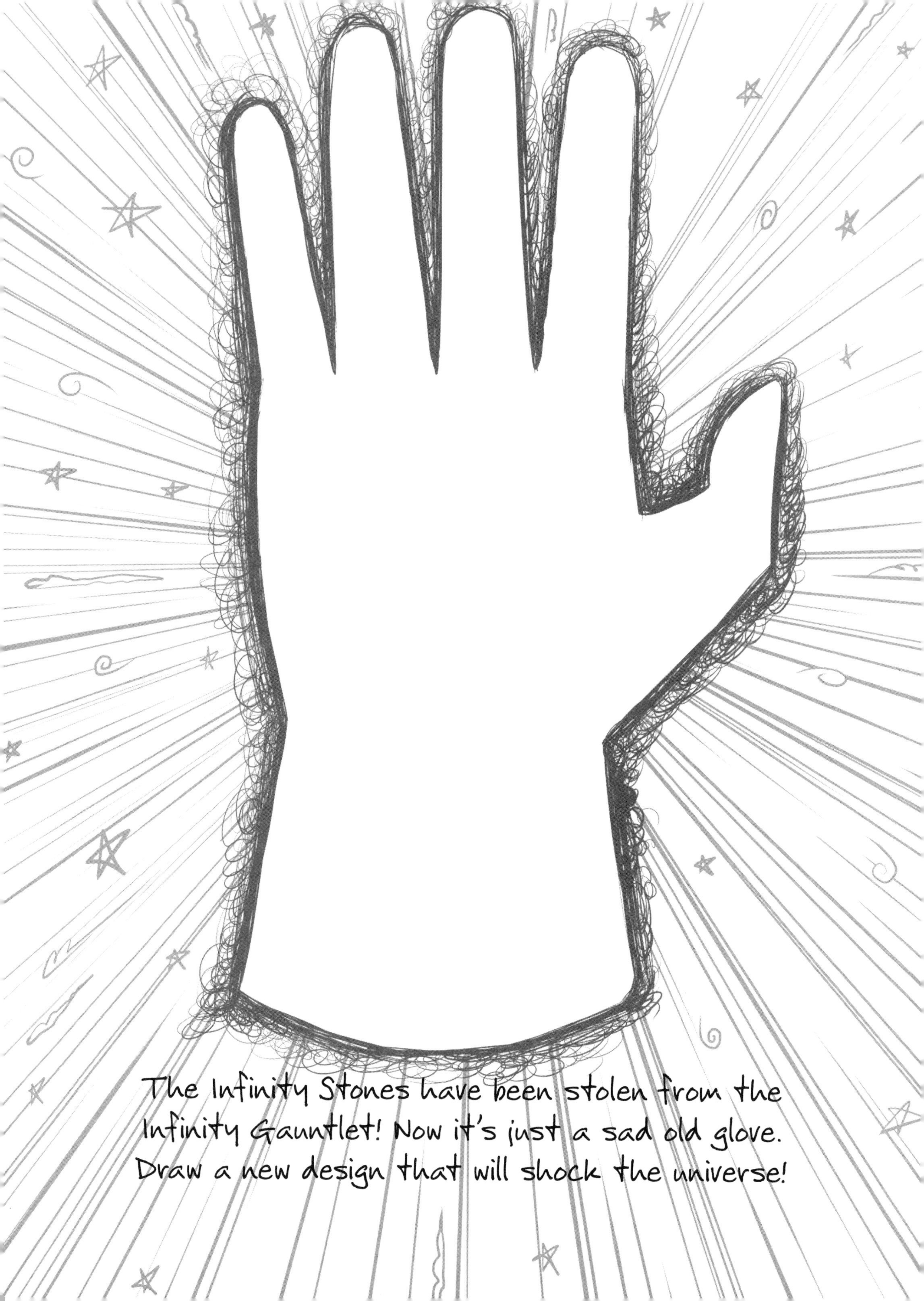

The Infinity Stones have been stolen from the Infinity Gauntlet! Now it's just a sad old glove. Draw a new design that will shock the universe!

Star-Lord got tangled up in his headphones AGAIN.
Draw a web of wires to keep him busy.

What the heck is going on here?!
Fill in the blank spaces to find out.

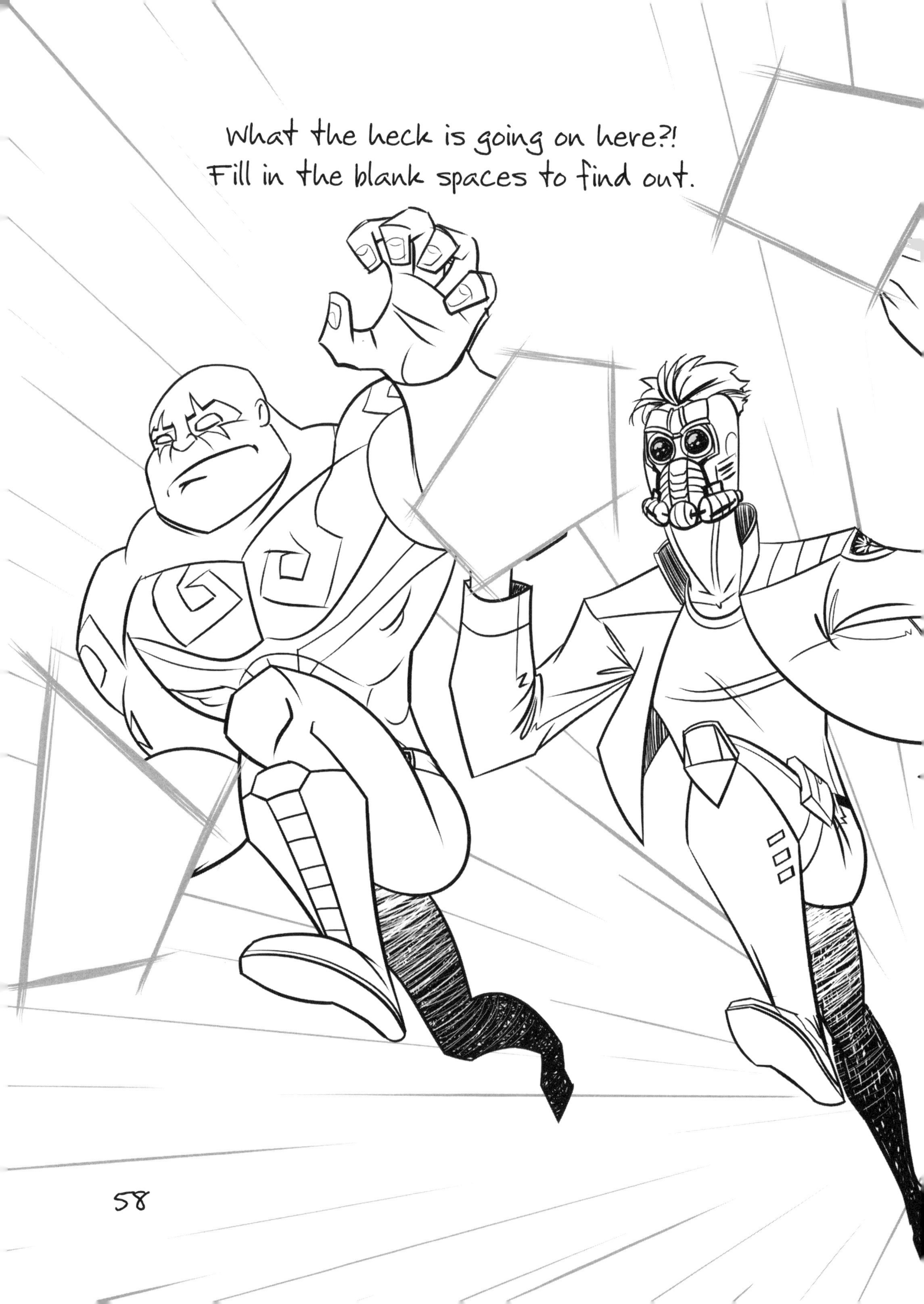

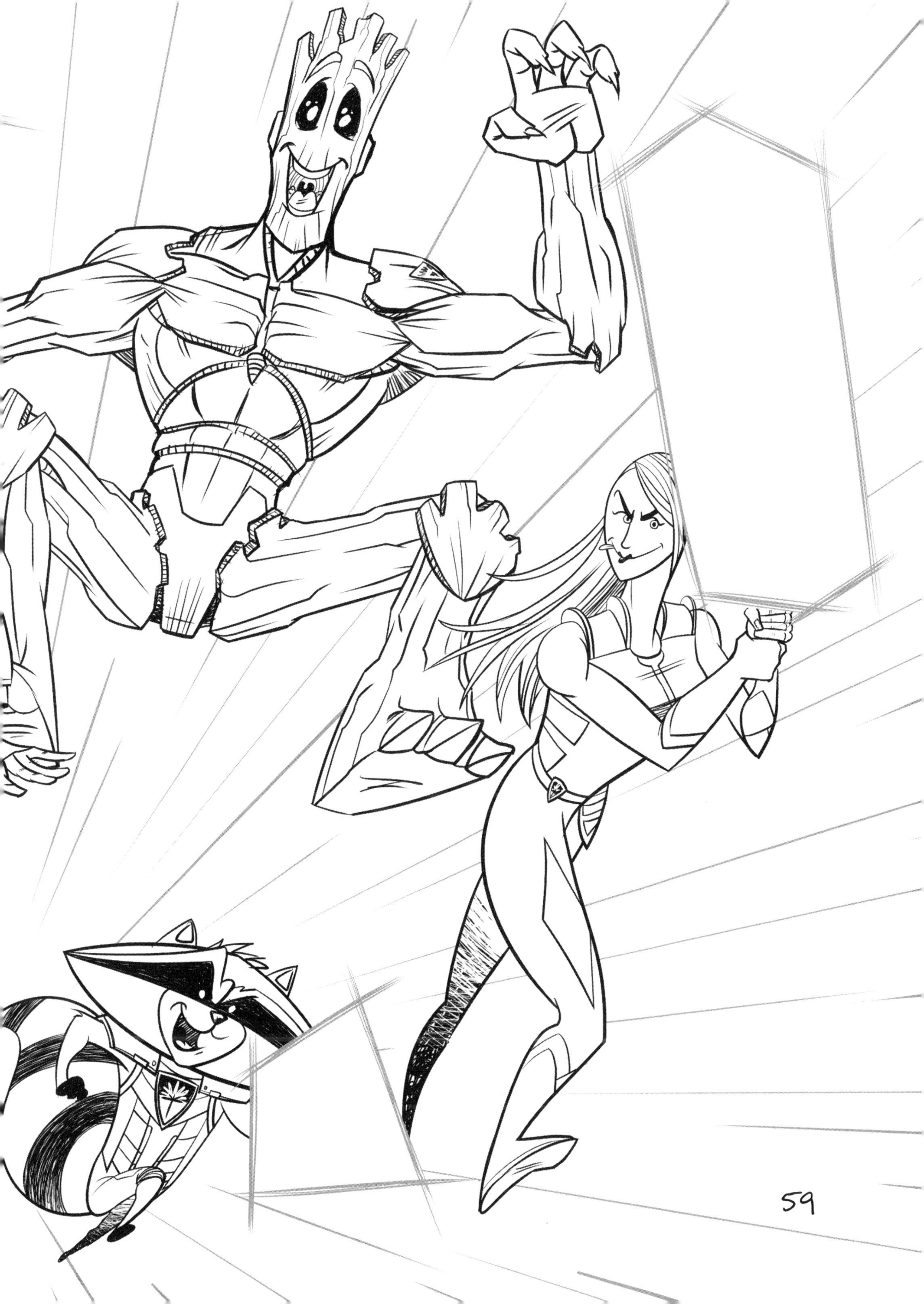

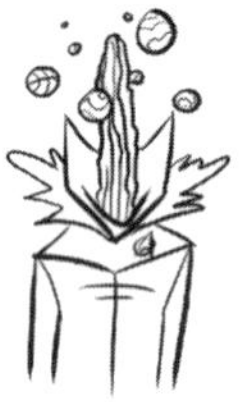

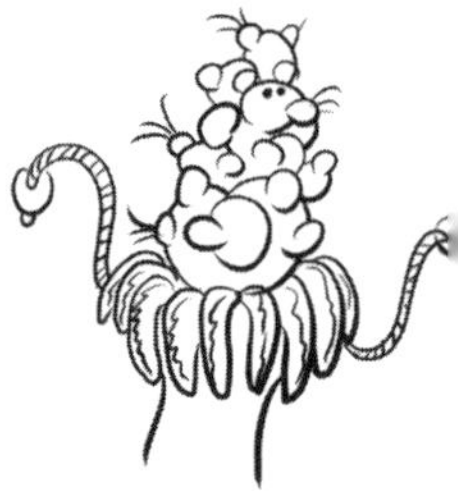

There's a whole stadium filled with the worst aliens in the galaxy. Looks like they want the Guardians to fight one another!

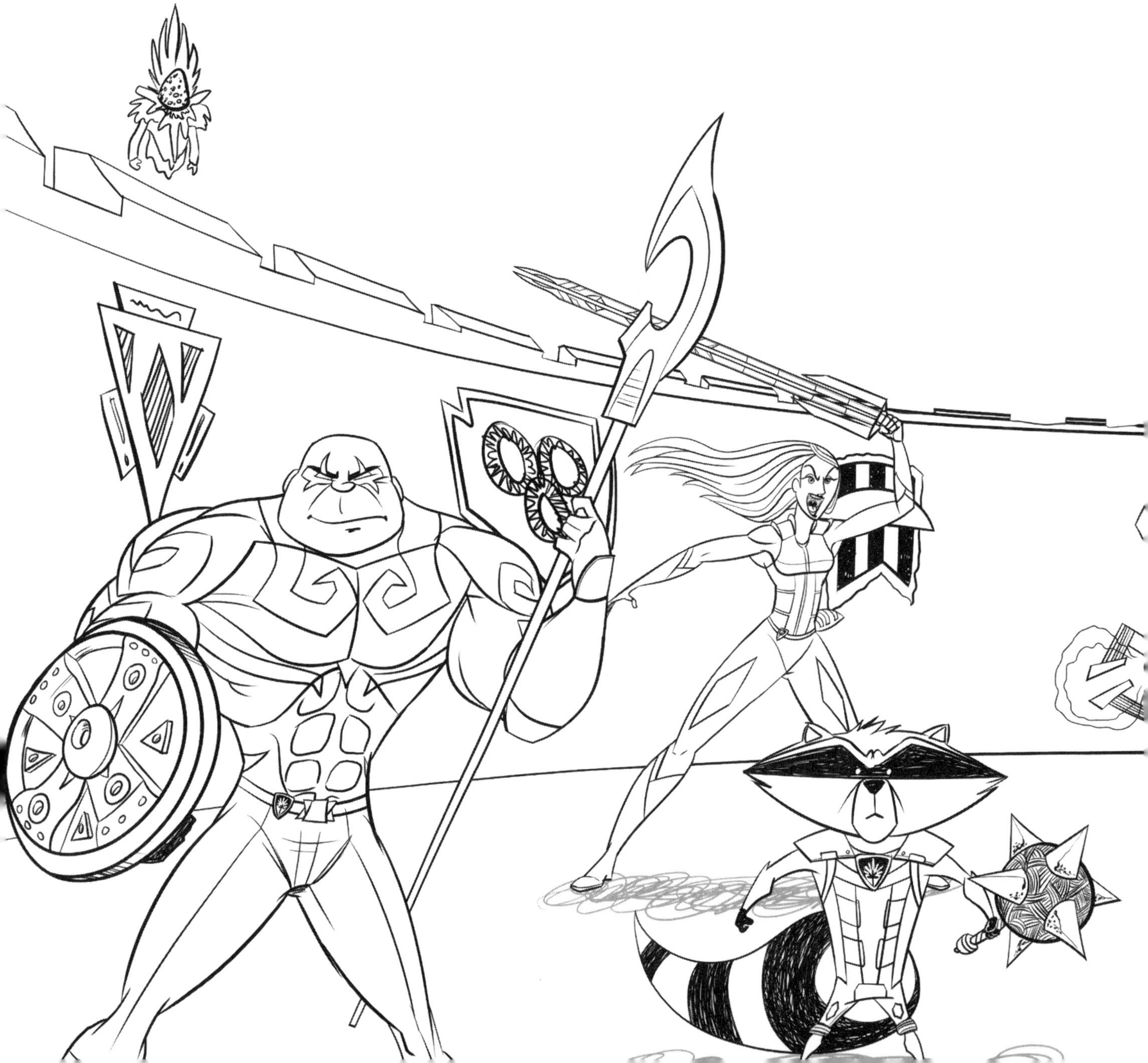

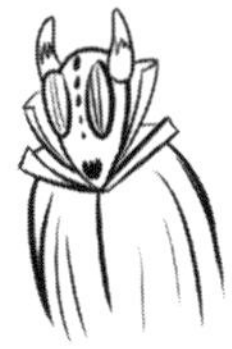

Draw some more of them and make
sure every seat is filled.

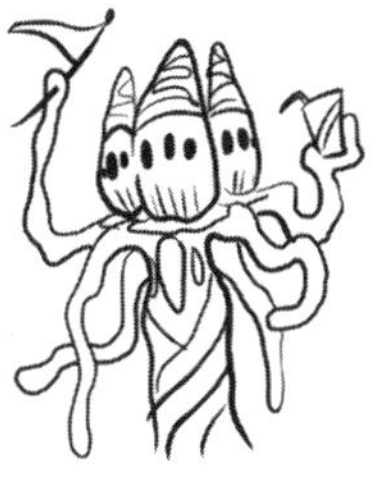

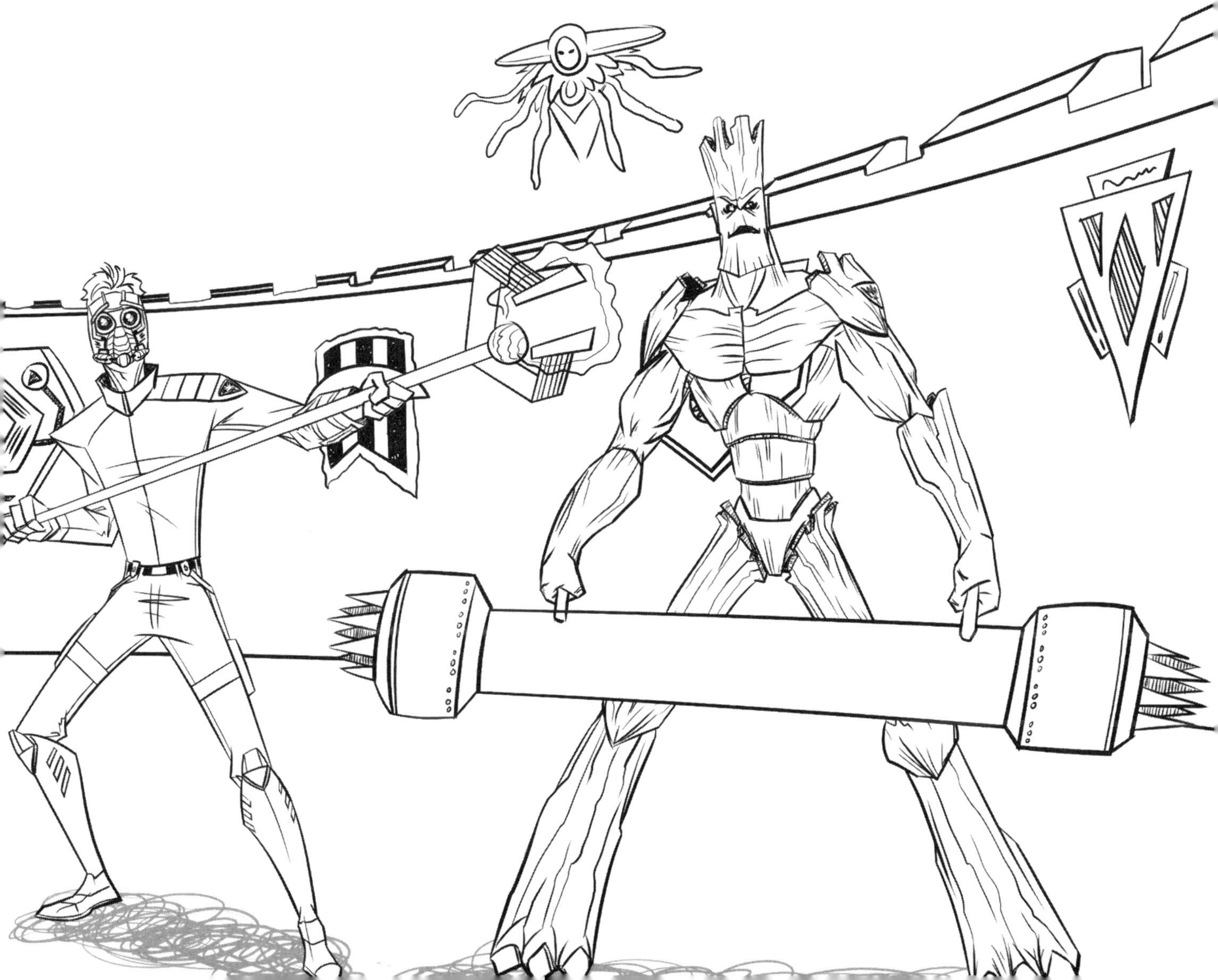

What if Groot were made entirely out of water?
DRAW IT!

What if Drax were teeny-tiny instead of big and bulky?
DRAW IT!

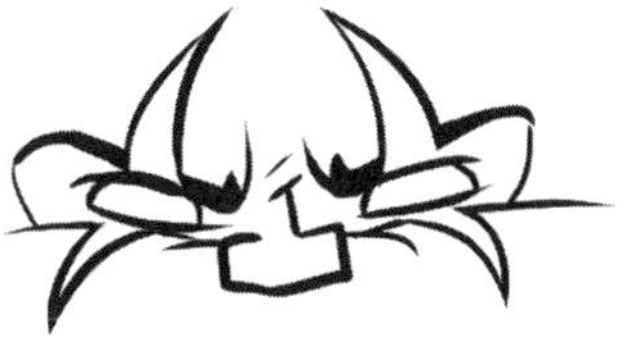

YUCK. Draw a creepy-crawly critter in Gamora's drink.

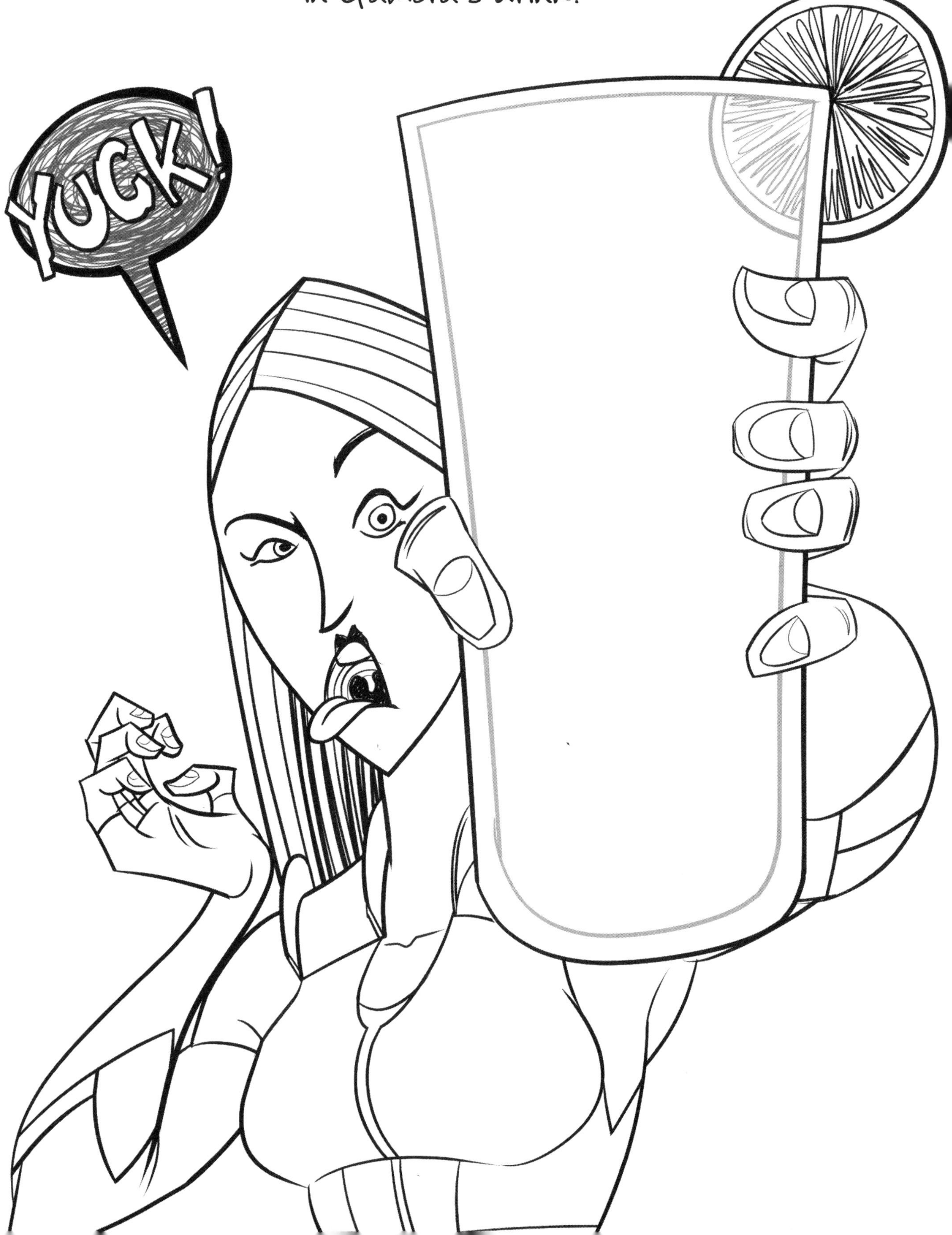
YUCK!

Rocket baked cupcakes with Drax's face on them.
Aww, that's sweet! OR IS IT?

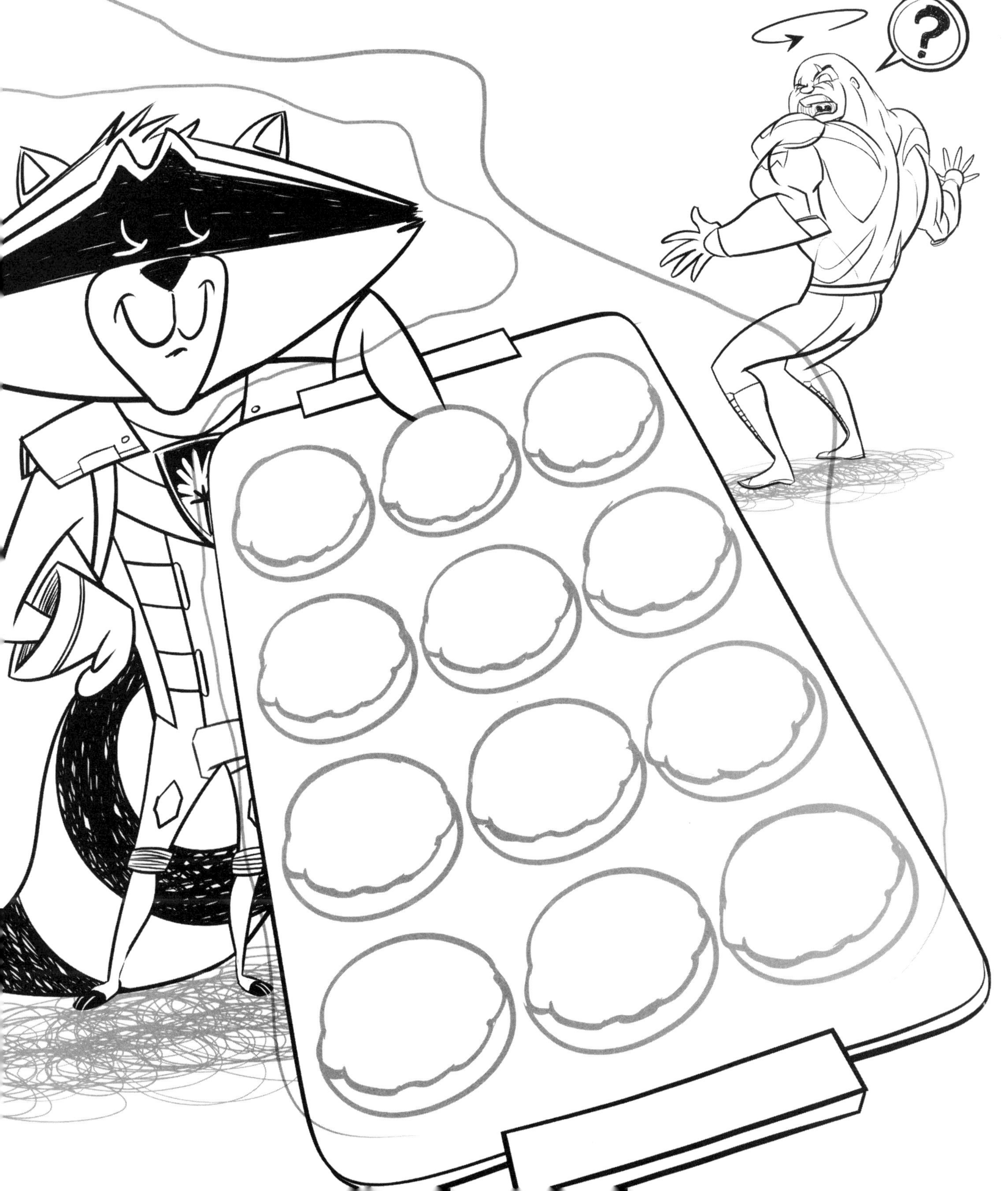
?

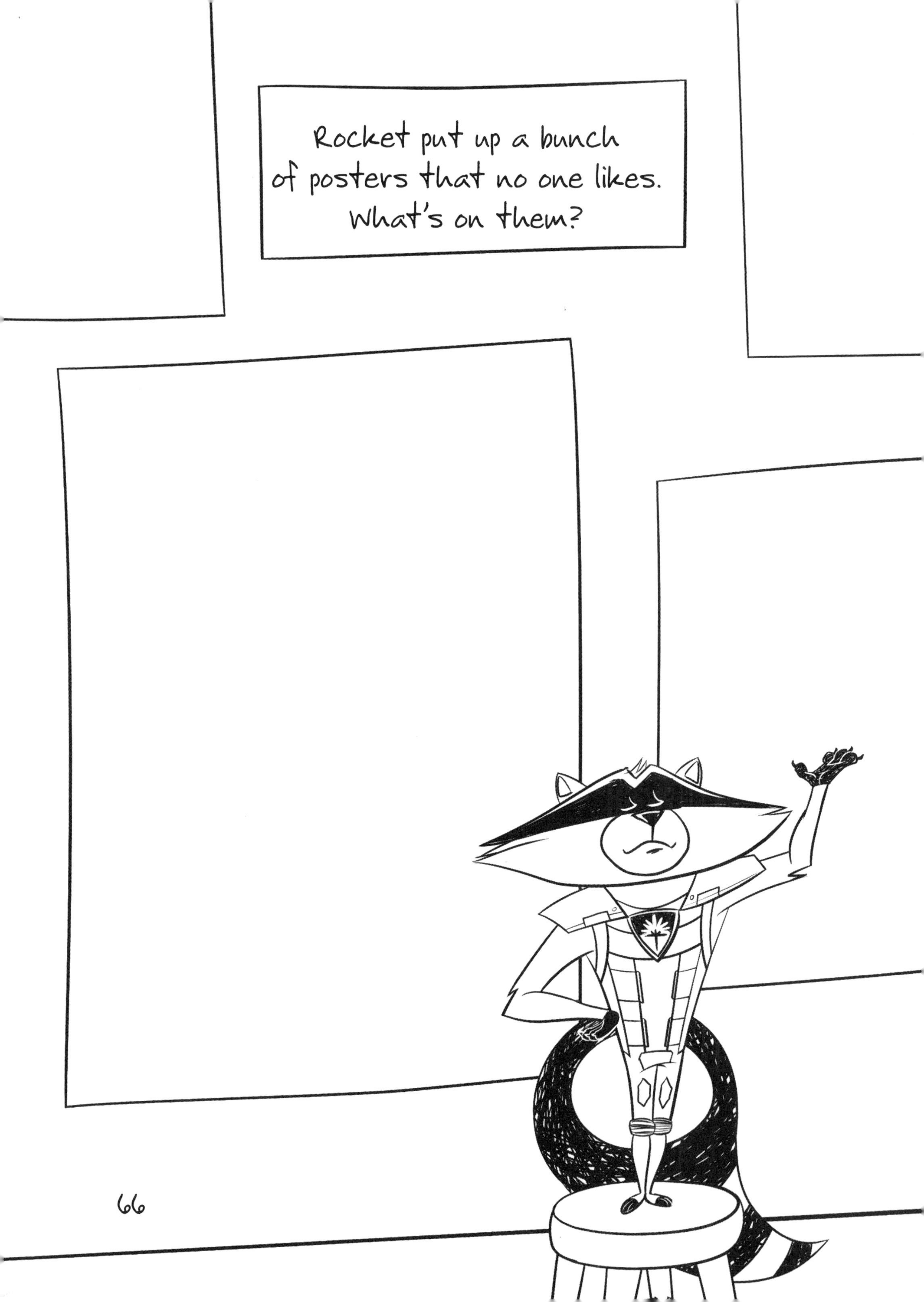
Rocket put up a bunch
of posters that no one likes.
What's on them?

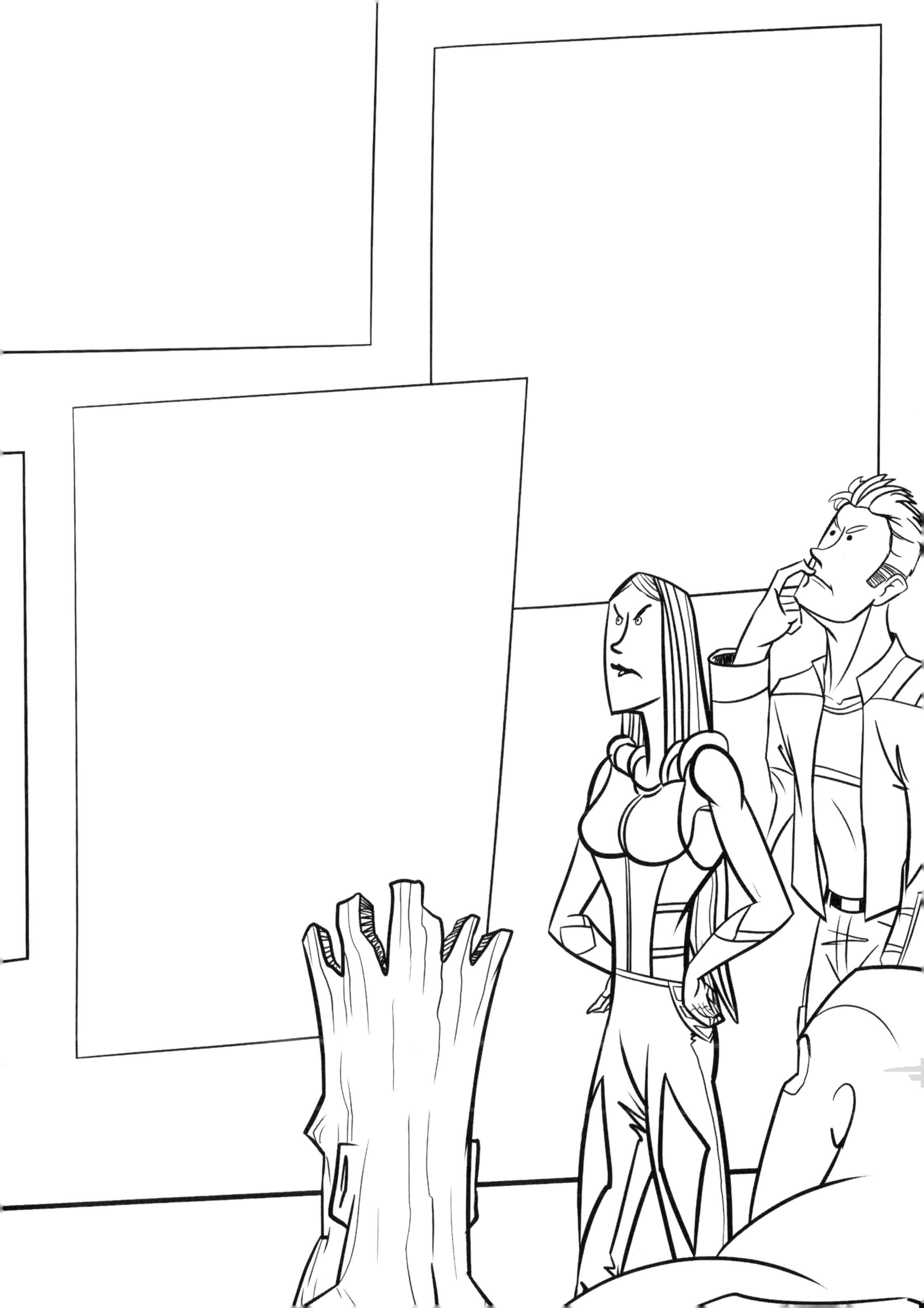

An eerie sea creature is swimming underneath
Rocket and Groot's boat. Draw it!

Hey, look! Yondu stopped
by to say hello. Give him
a wild and crazy Mohawk
and maybe some balloons,
too, since he looks like he
needs some cheering up.

Gamora is so excited! She just can't hide it.
Draw her enthusiastic face.

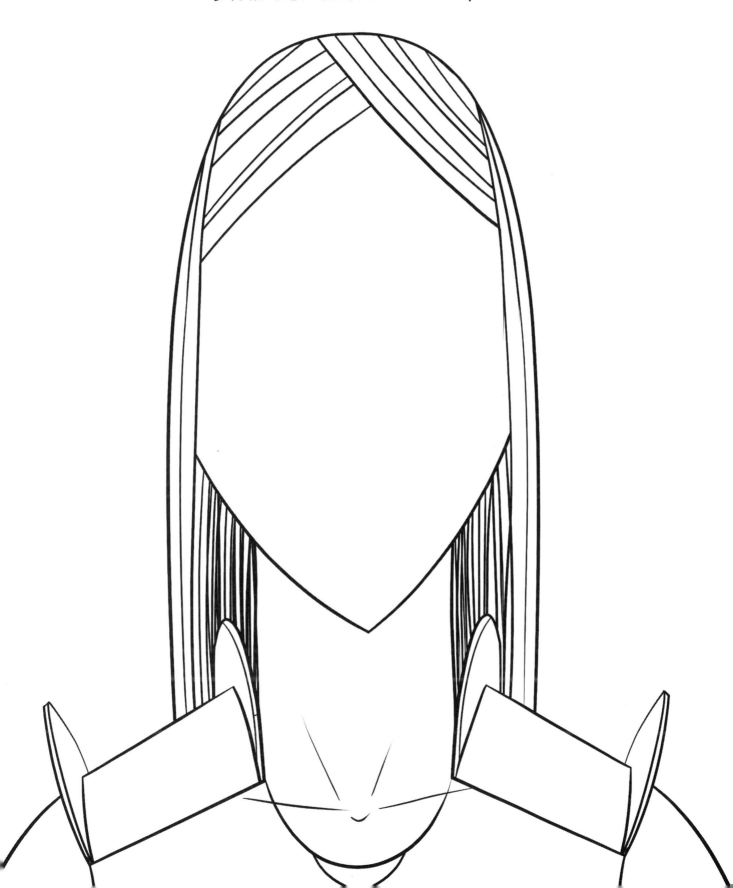

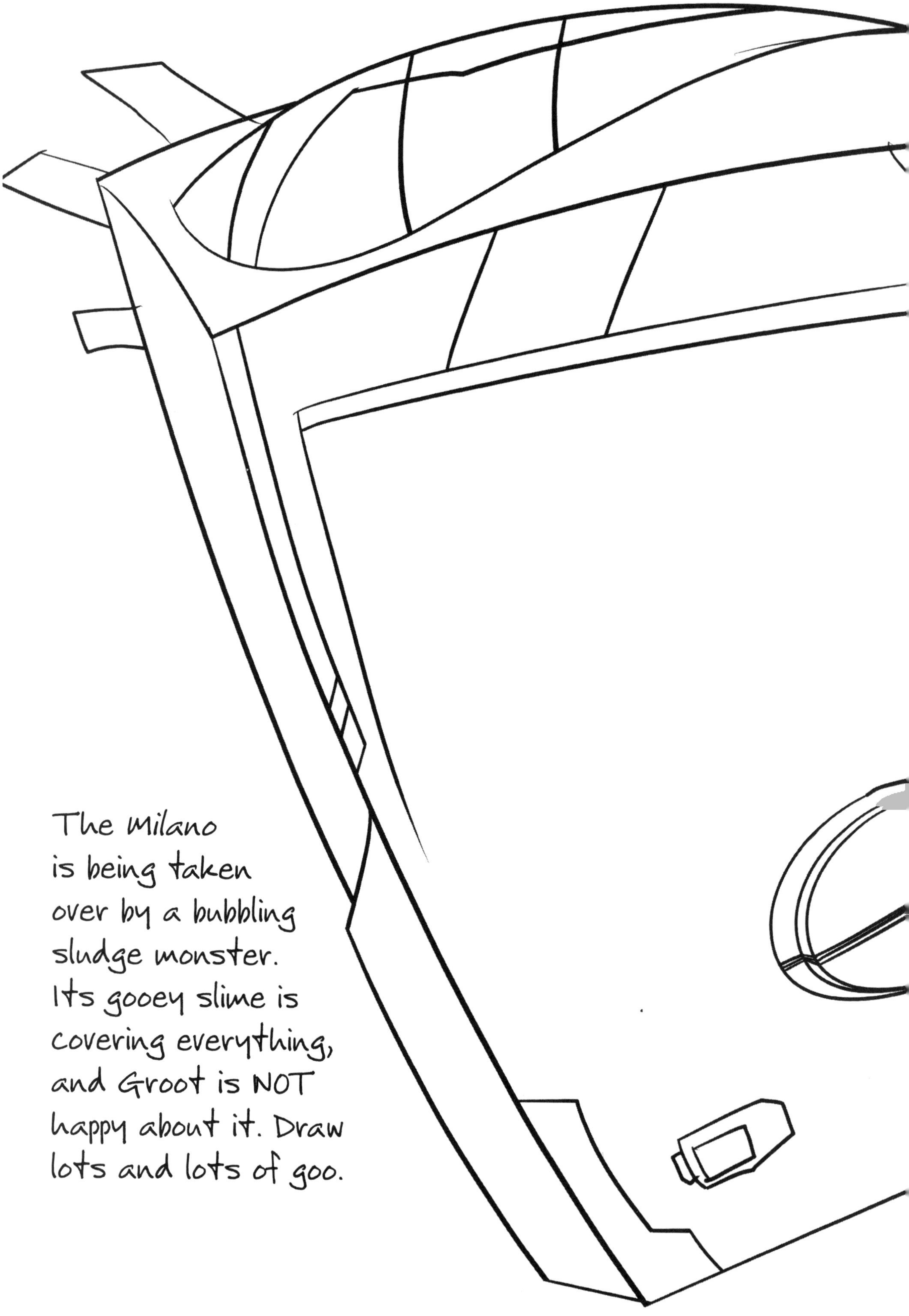

The Milano
is being taken
over by a bubbling
sludge monster.
Its gooey slime is
covering everything,
and Groot is NOT
happy about it. Draw
lots and lots of goo.

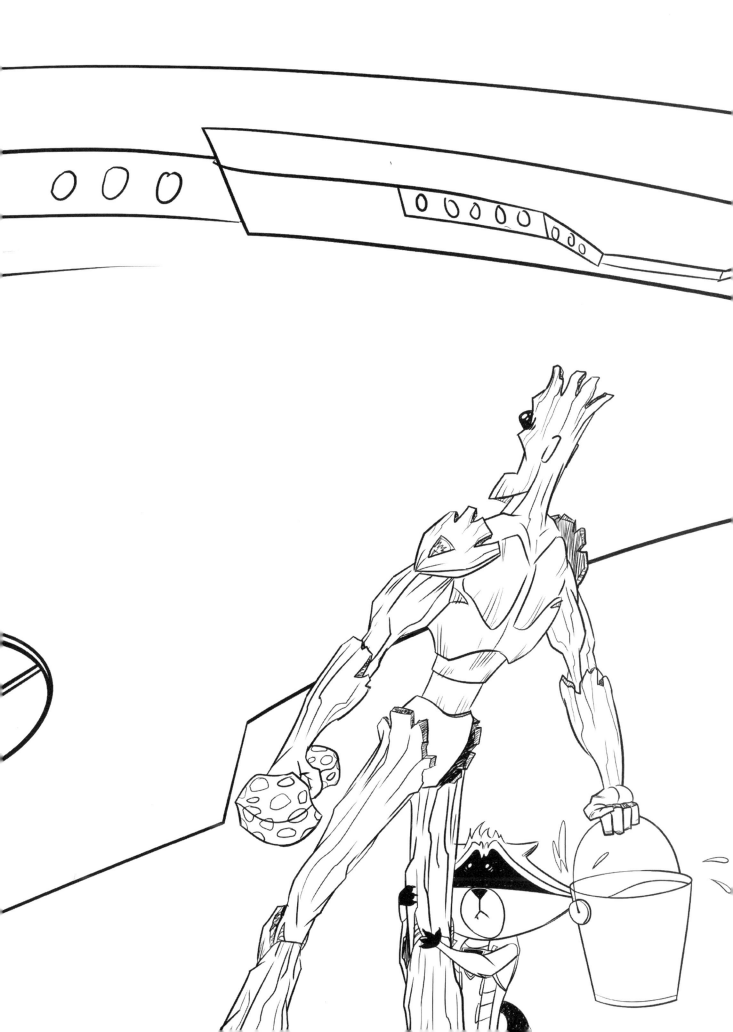

Give Rocket the biggest, baddest laser blaster in the entire flarking galaxy.

Drax sleeps with a very creepy doll.
Don't tell anyone! It's a secret.
Draw him a ghoulish little dolly.

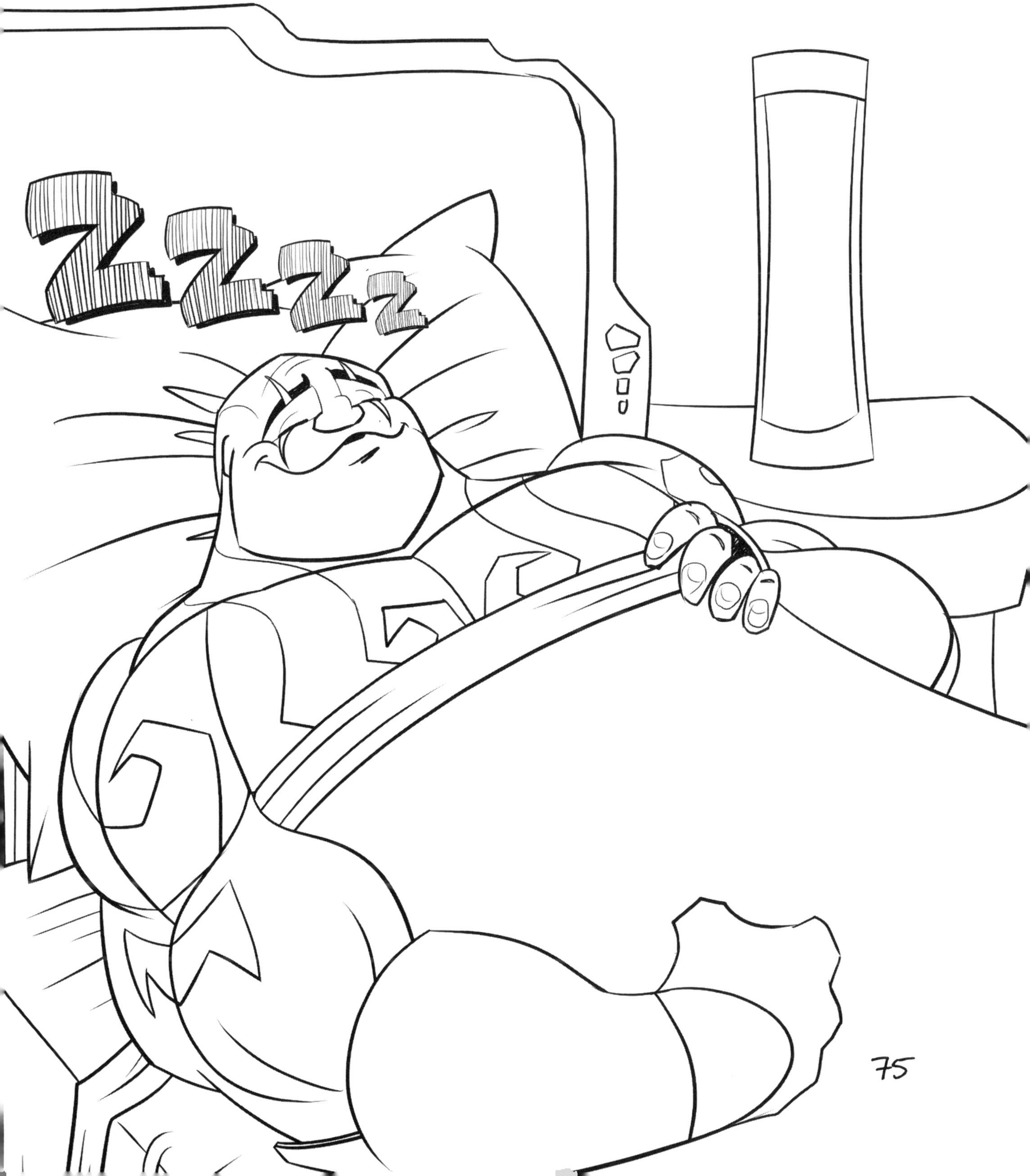
Zzzz

Groot accidentally brought an alien beehive onto the Milano and now a swarm of space bees is terrorizing everyone.

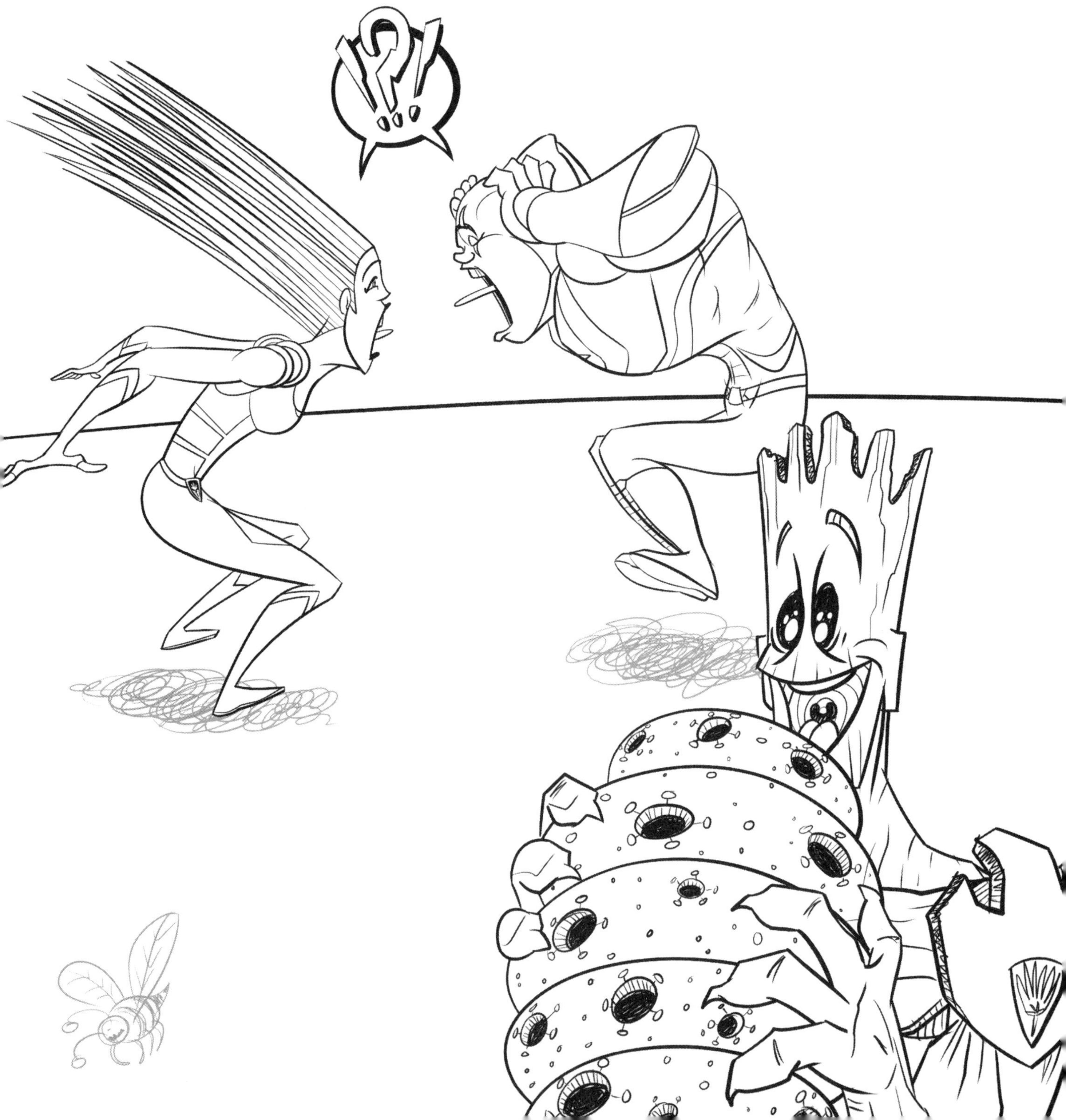
!?!

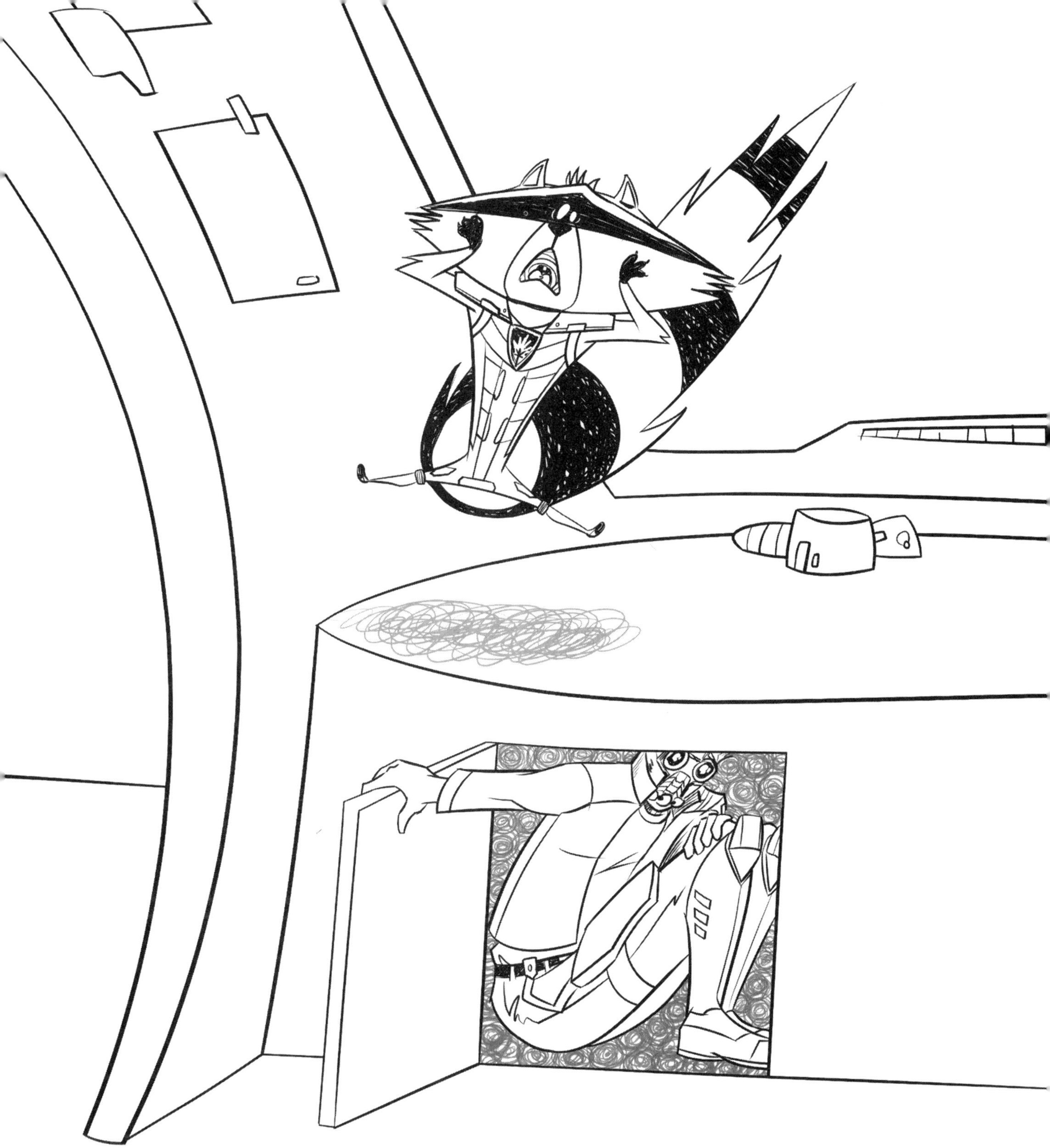

Draw lots of bees. BIG bees. Small bees.
BEES! BEES! BEES!

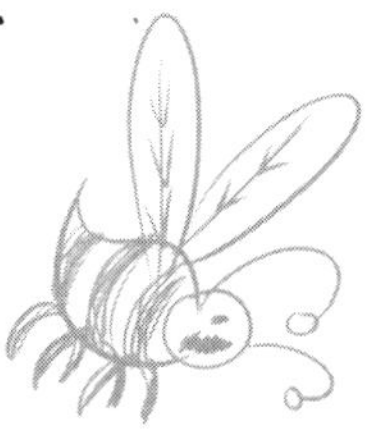

Gamora is NOT a fan of wearing dresses.
But draw her one anyway, just this once.

The Collector REALLY wants to sell off this old monster, but no one seems to want to buy it. Why is that?

Draw a monster that no one is interested in.

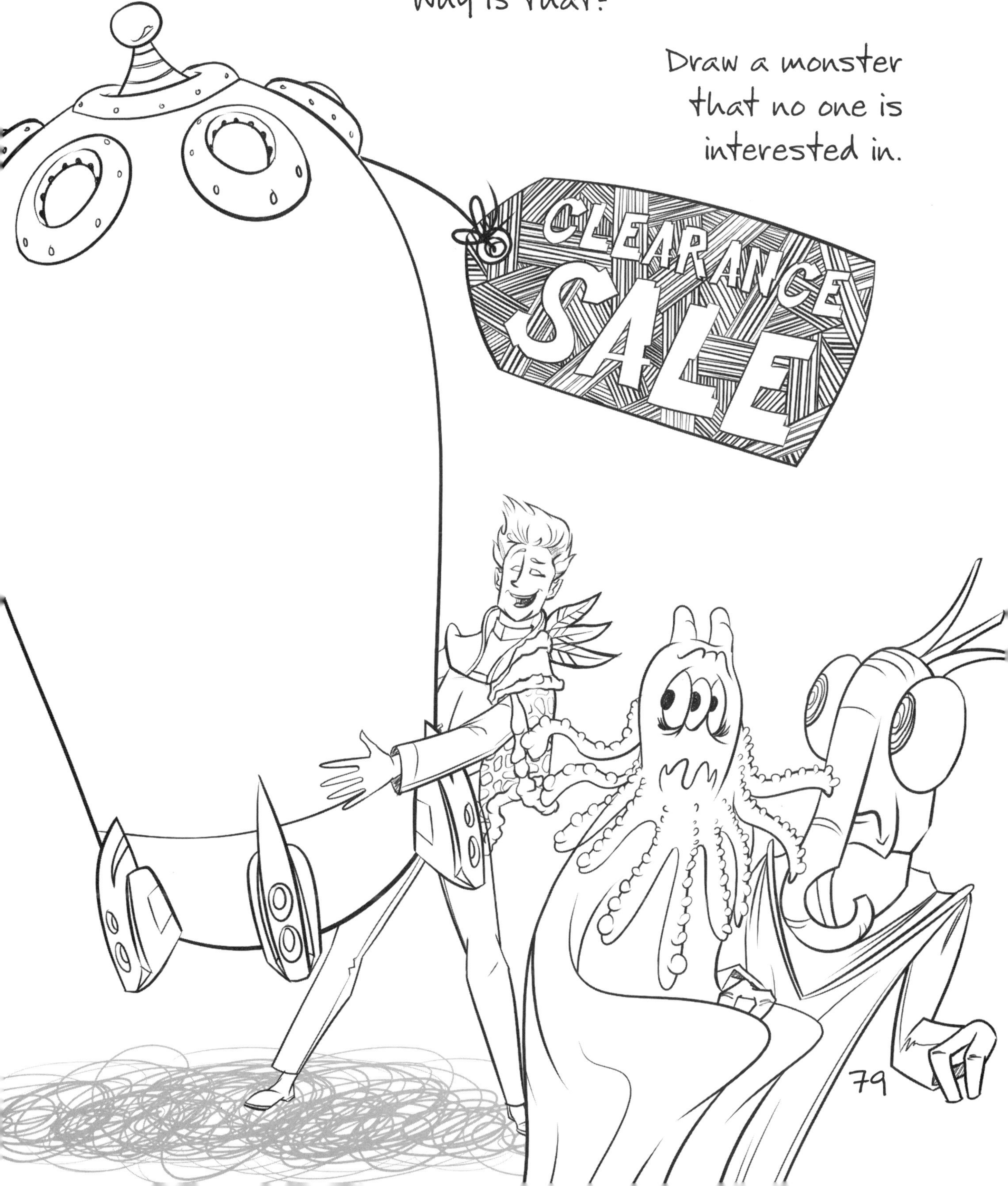
CLEARANCE SALE

What is Rocket smelling?!
Whatever it is, make sure it's
big and stinky.

Star-Lord made Groot the most
incredible sandwich in the entire galaxy.
Draw its delicious glory!

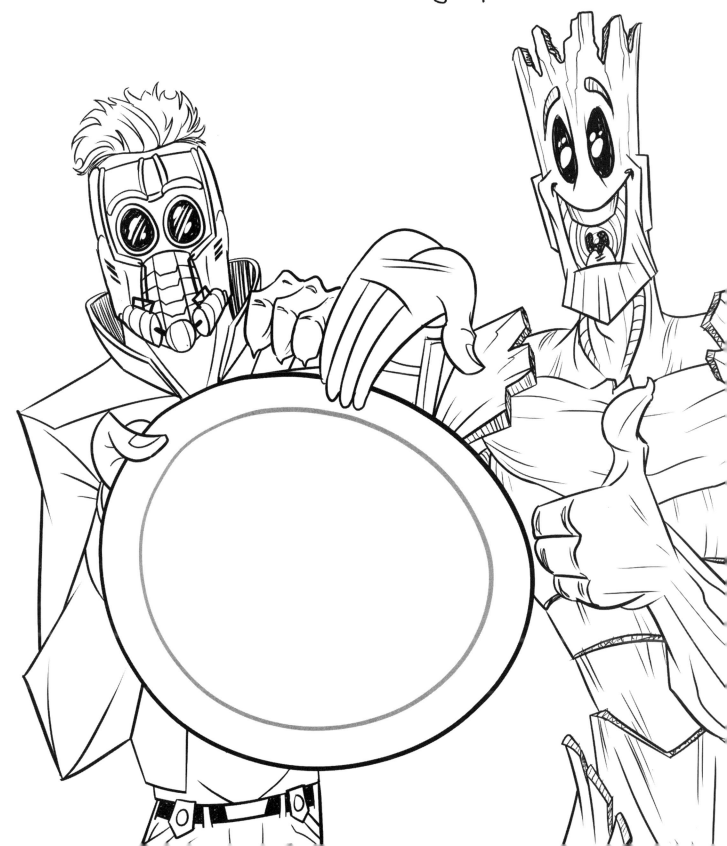

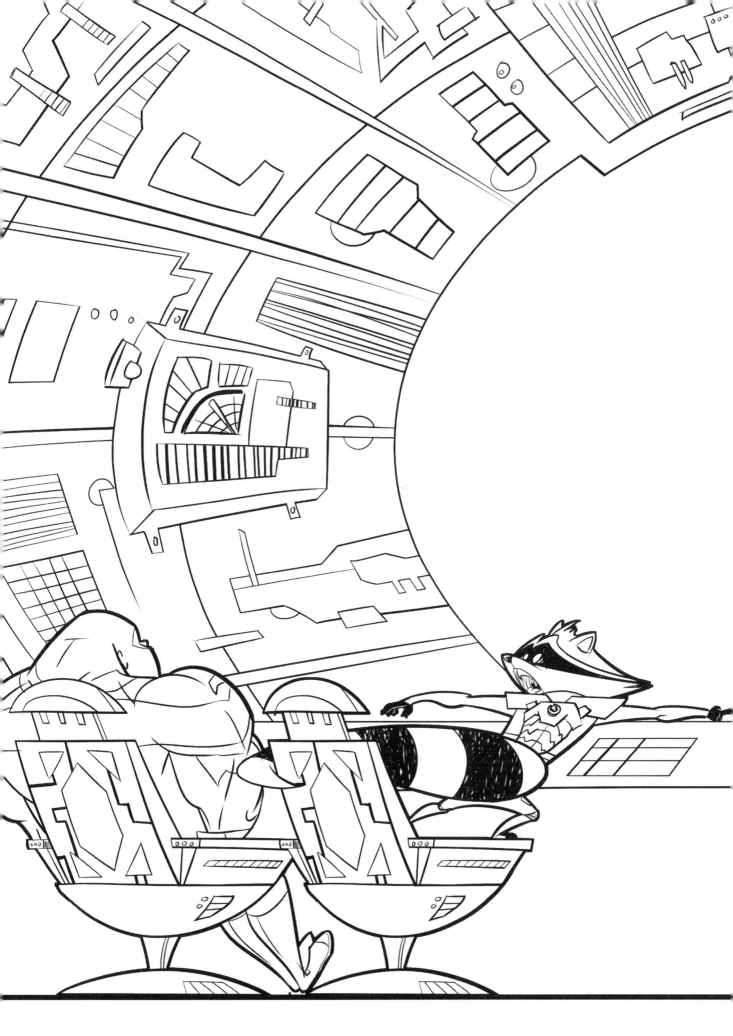

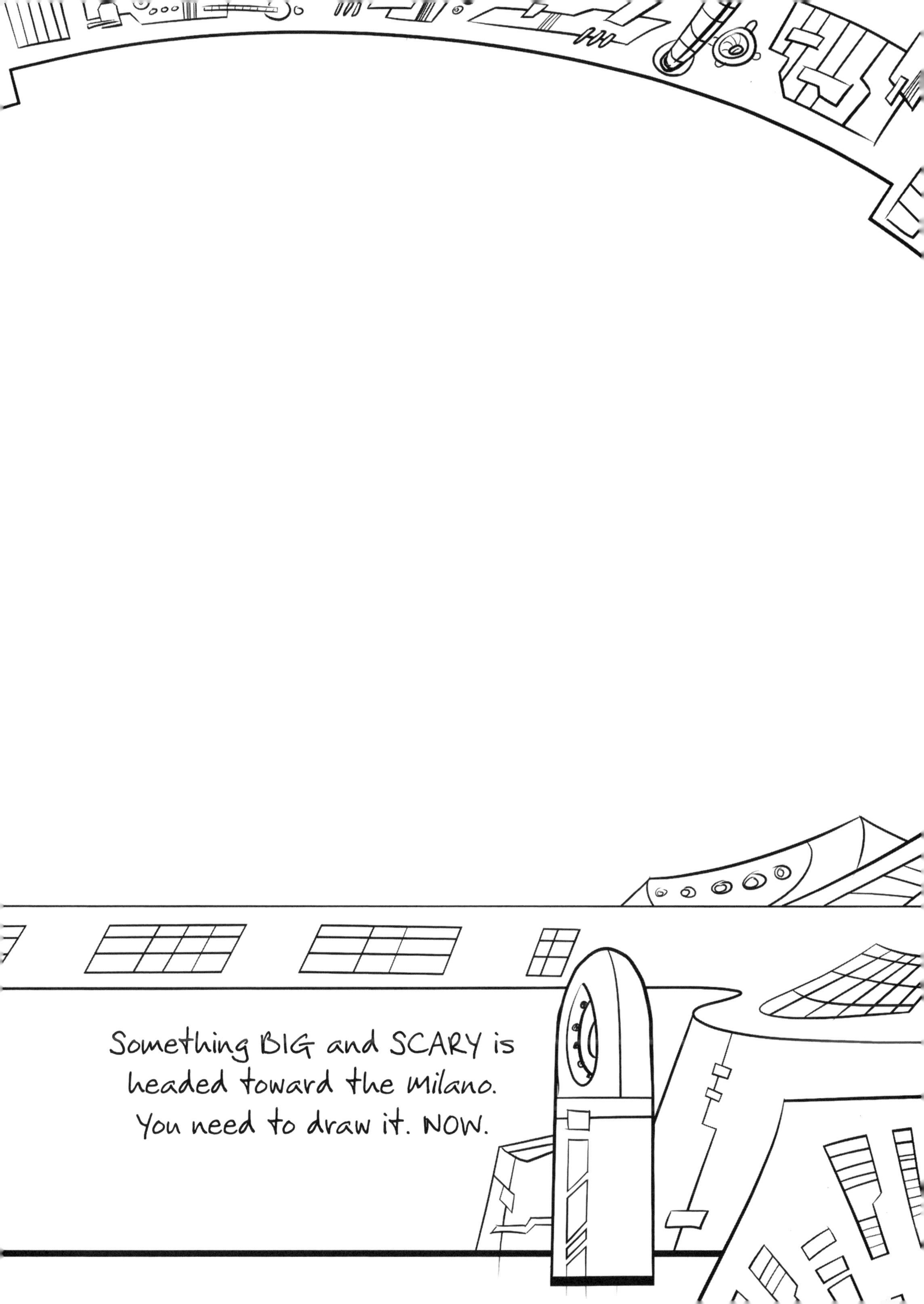
Something BIG and SCARY is headed toward the Milano. You need to draw it. NOW.

The Guardians have uncovered an ancient book of secrets. This is NOT GOOD.
What's it called? What does it look like?

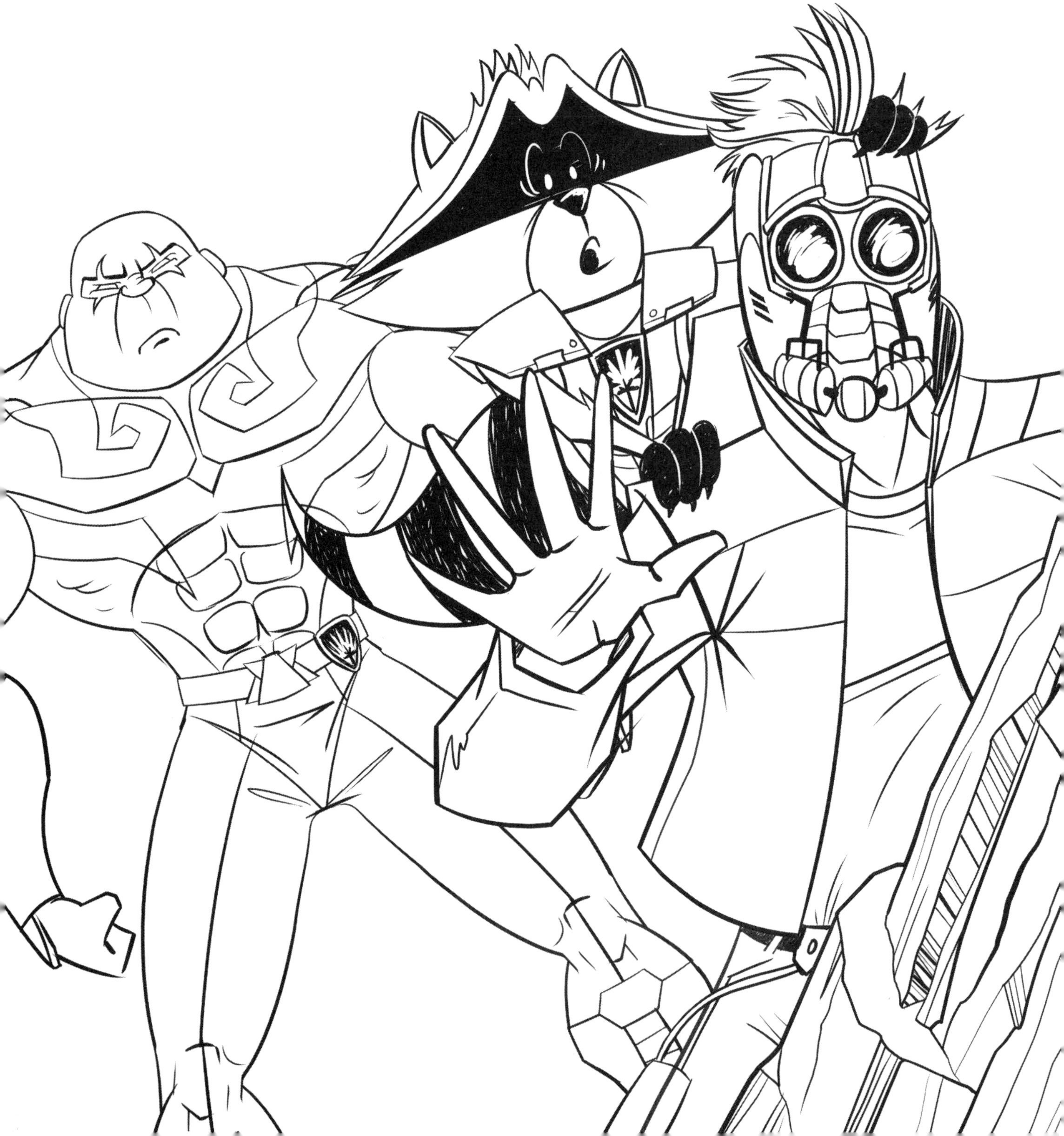

Decorate it with some ancient hieroglyphics while you're at it.

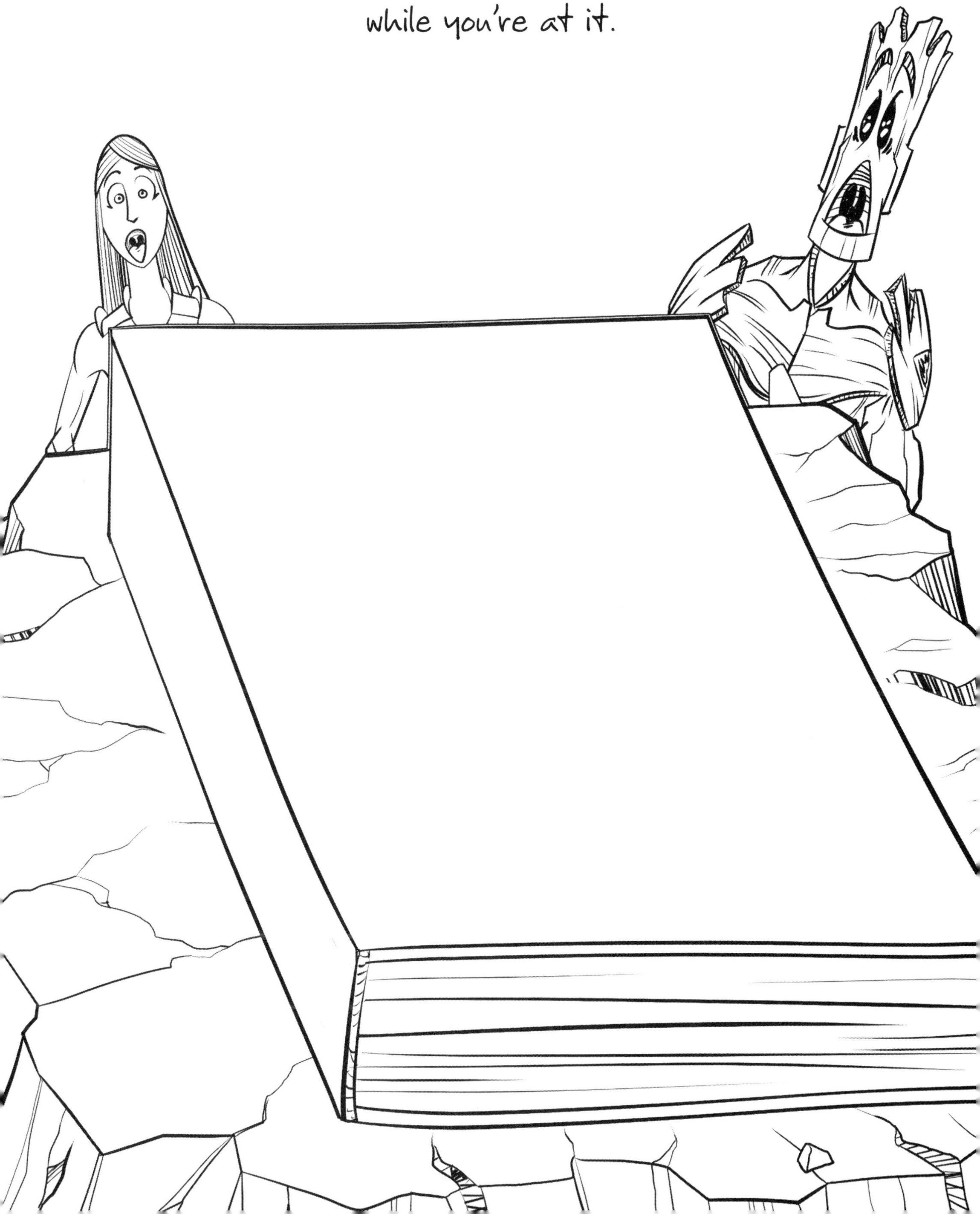

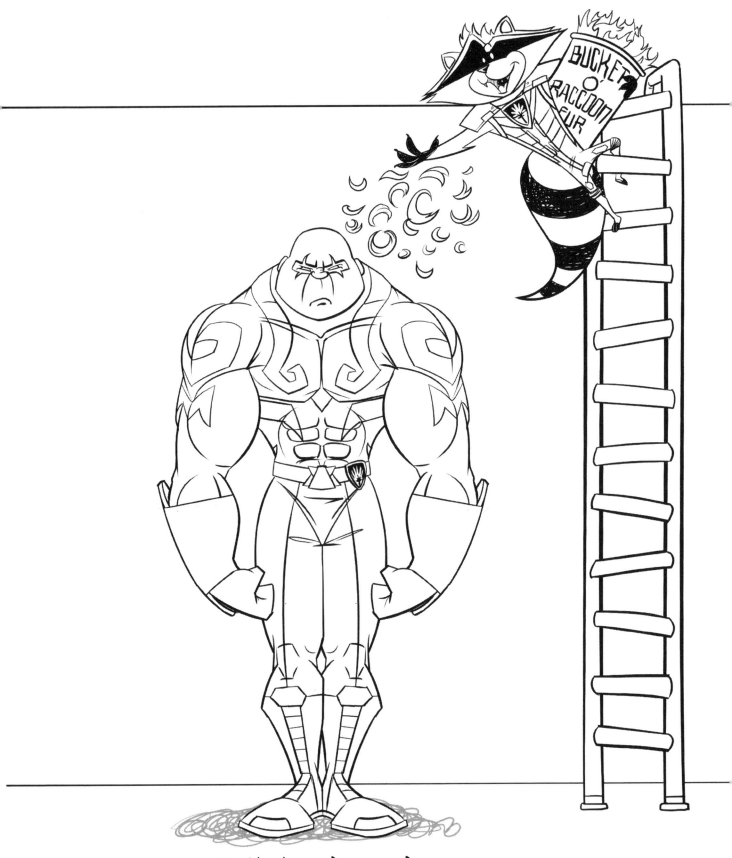

Wouldn't it be funny if Drax were
actually furry like Rocket?
Cover him in raccoon fur. He'll love it.

What is Thanos holding?
Whatever it is, make
sure it's EVIL.

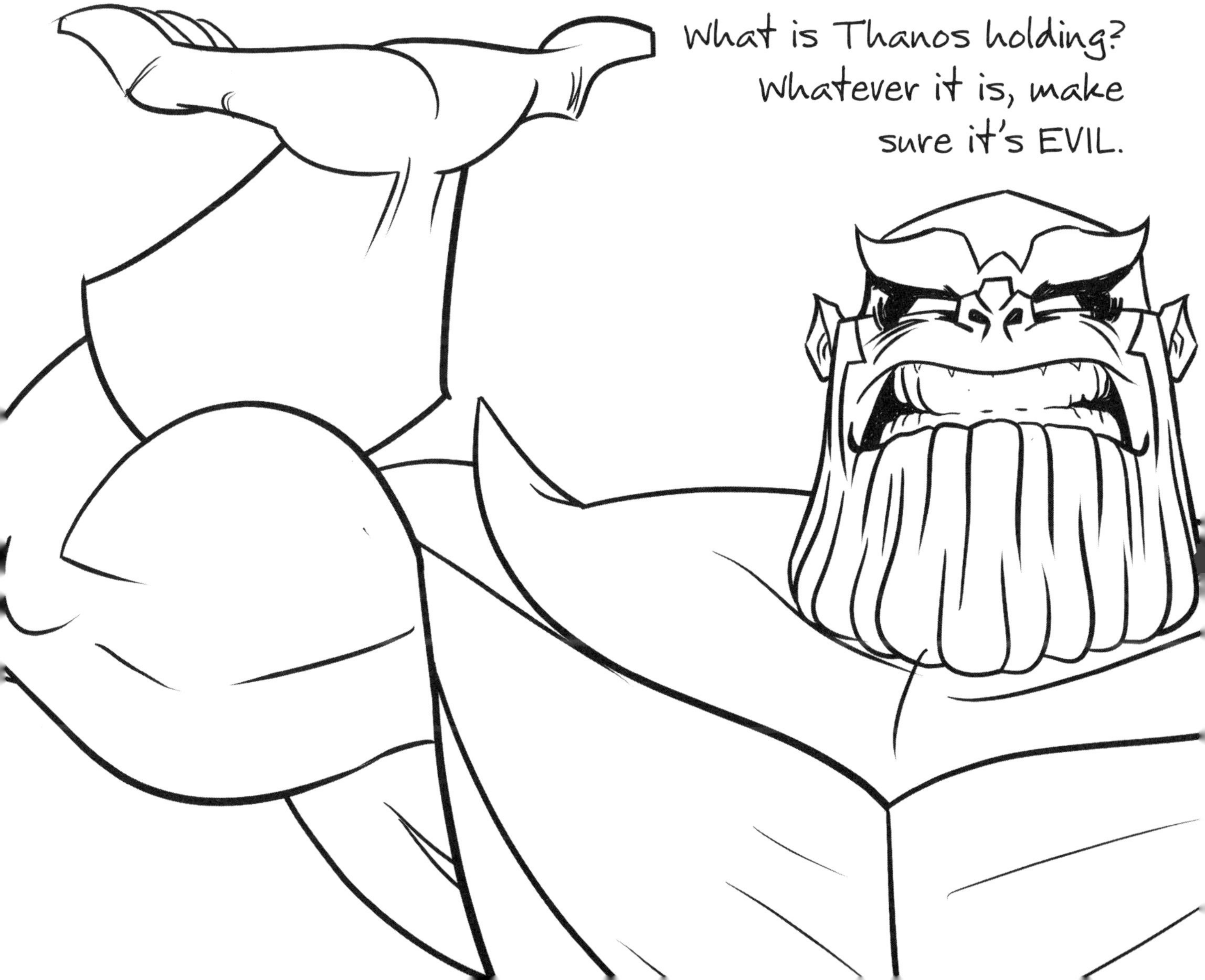

Drax is having a little trouble figuring out how to fly the Milano. Draw lots of levers, monitors, gauges, buttons, and switches on the control panel.

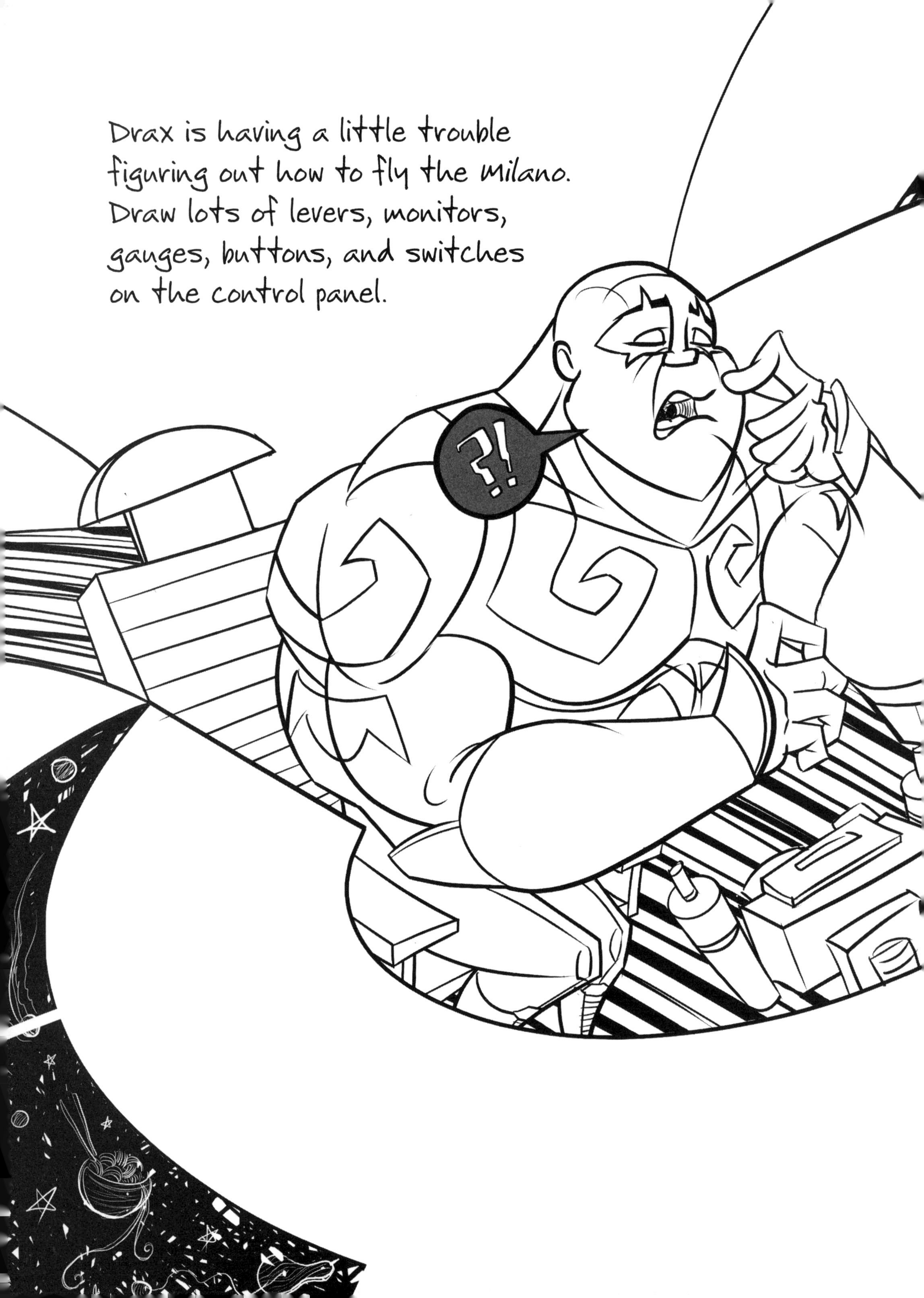
?!

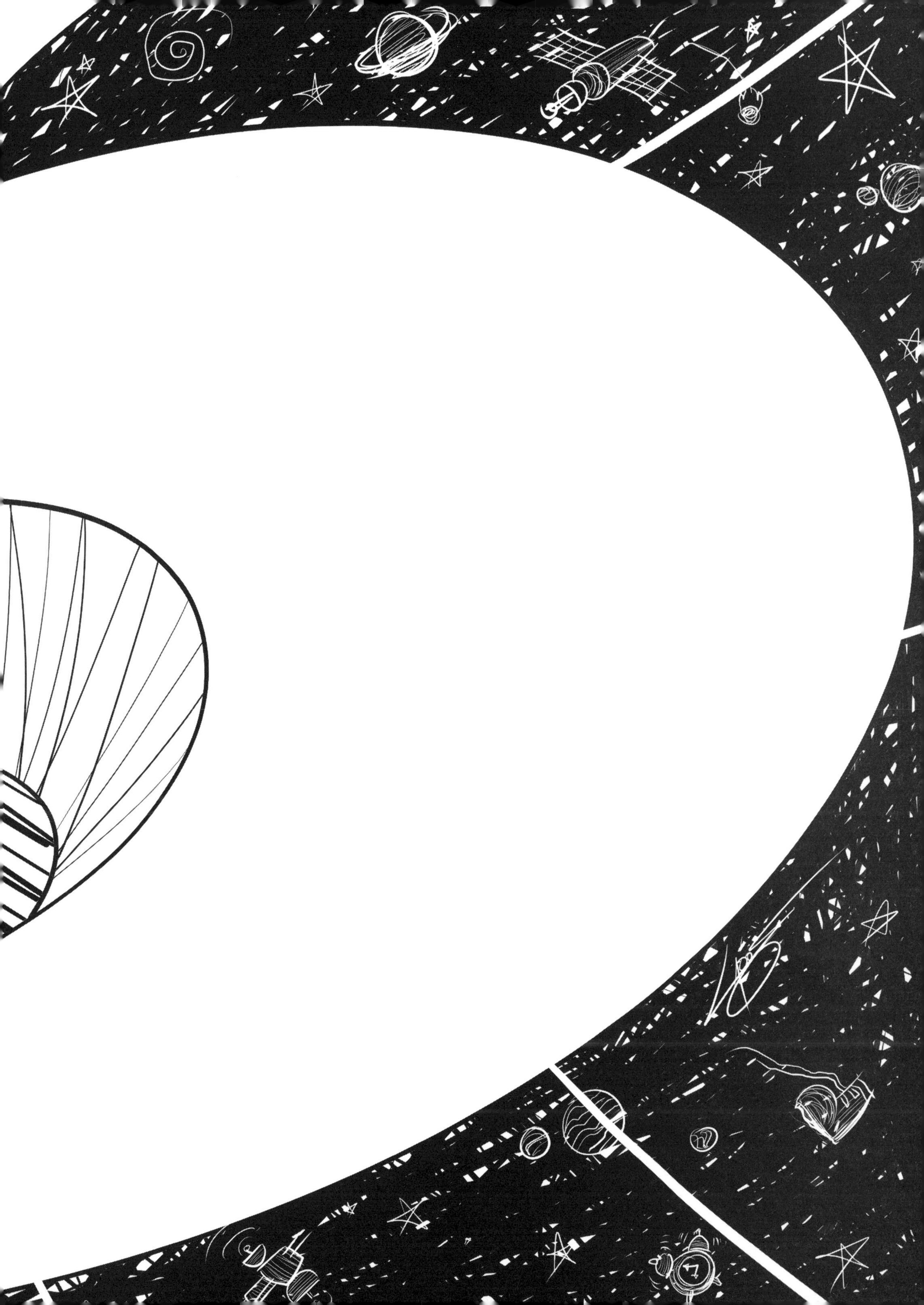

Draw Rocket's head on Groot's body
and Groot's head on Rocket's body.

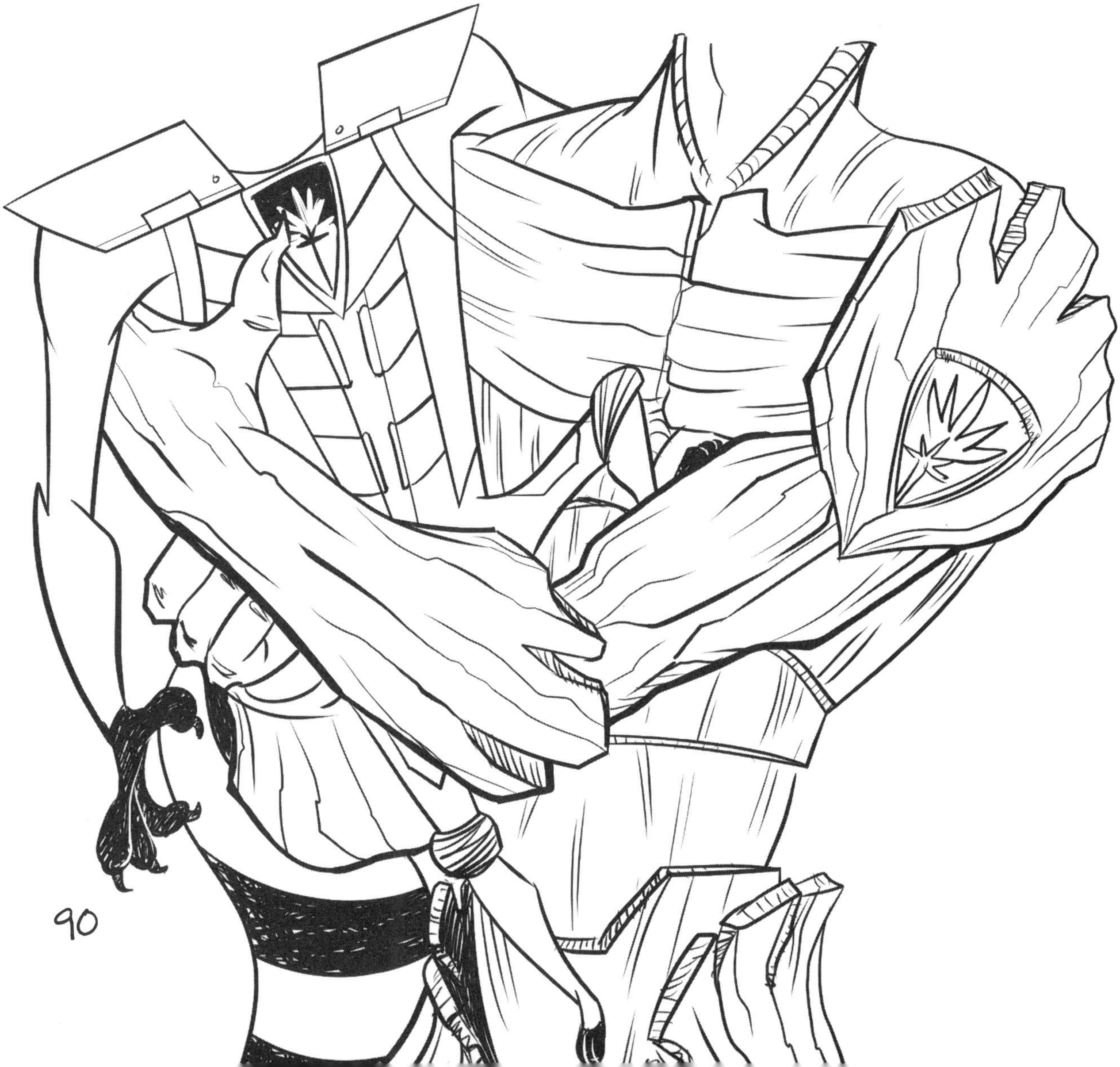

Star-Lord's mask needs a little upgrade.
Draw a nifty new version with lots of cool stuff!

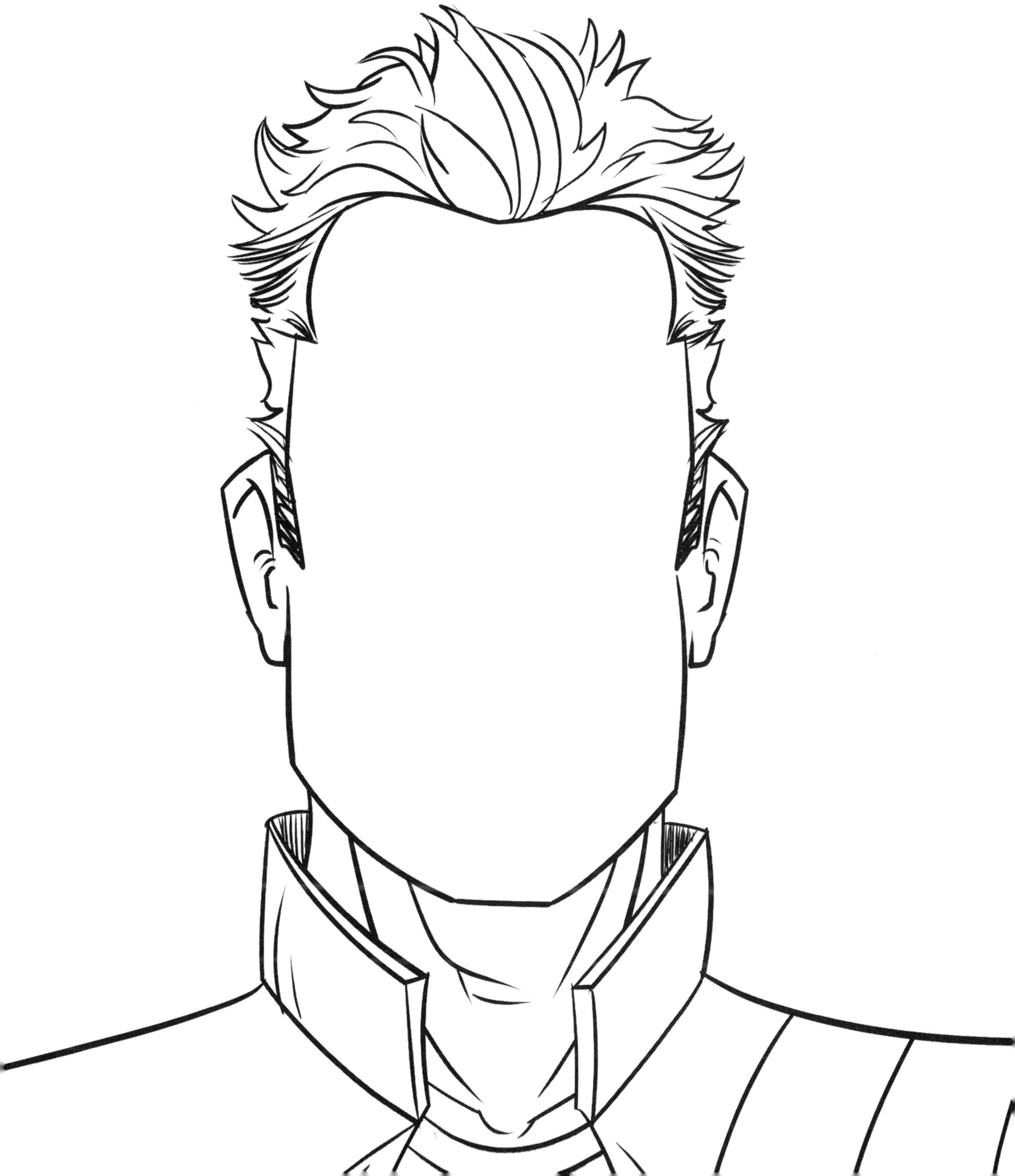

Wouldn't it be funny if Groot wore clothes?
Draw him a swanky outfit.

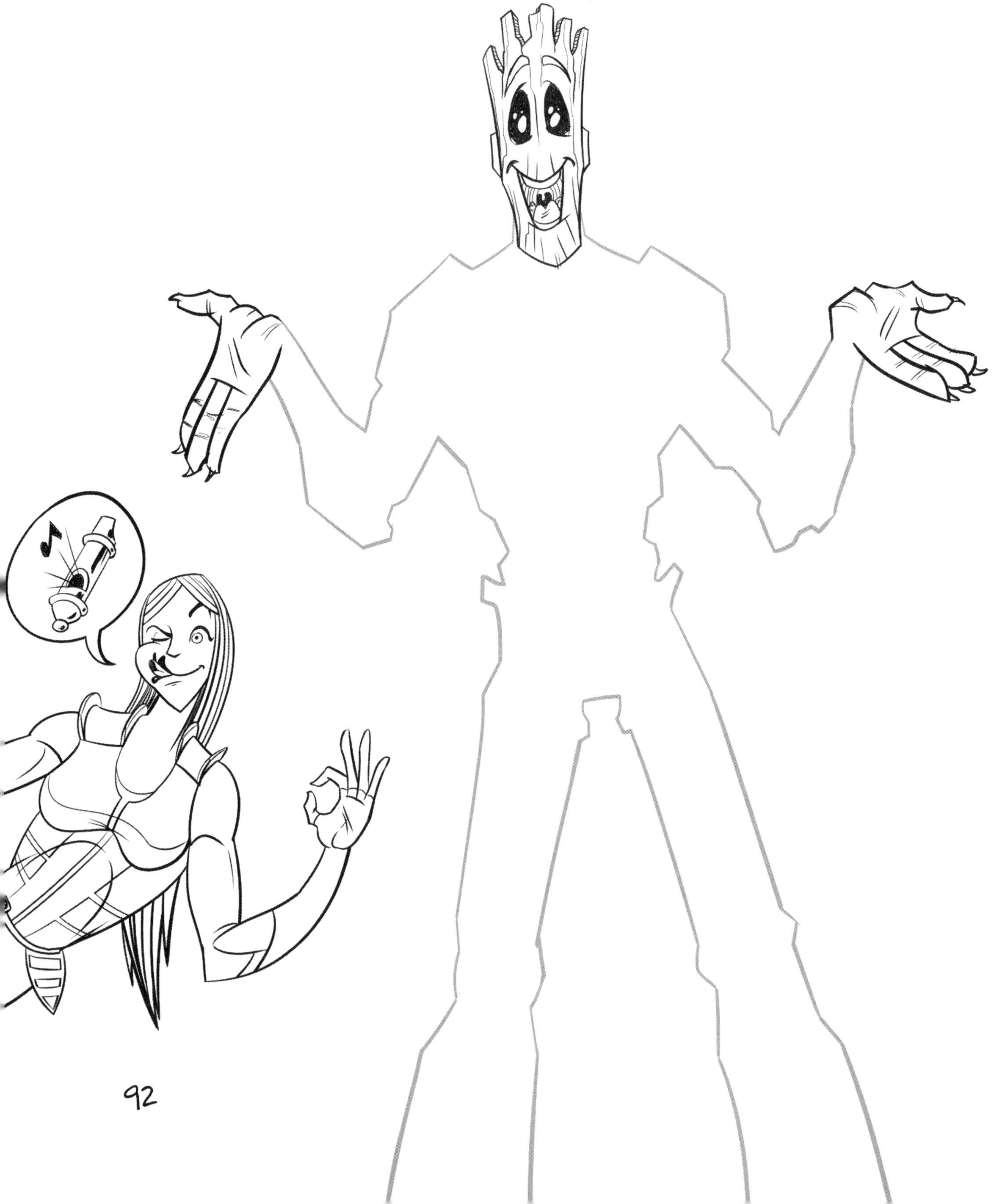

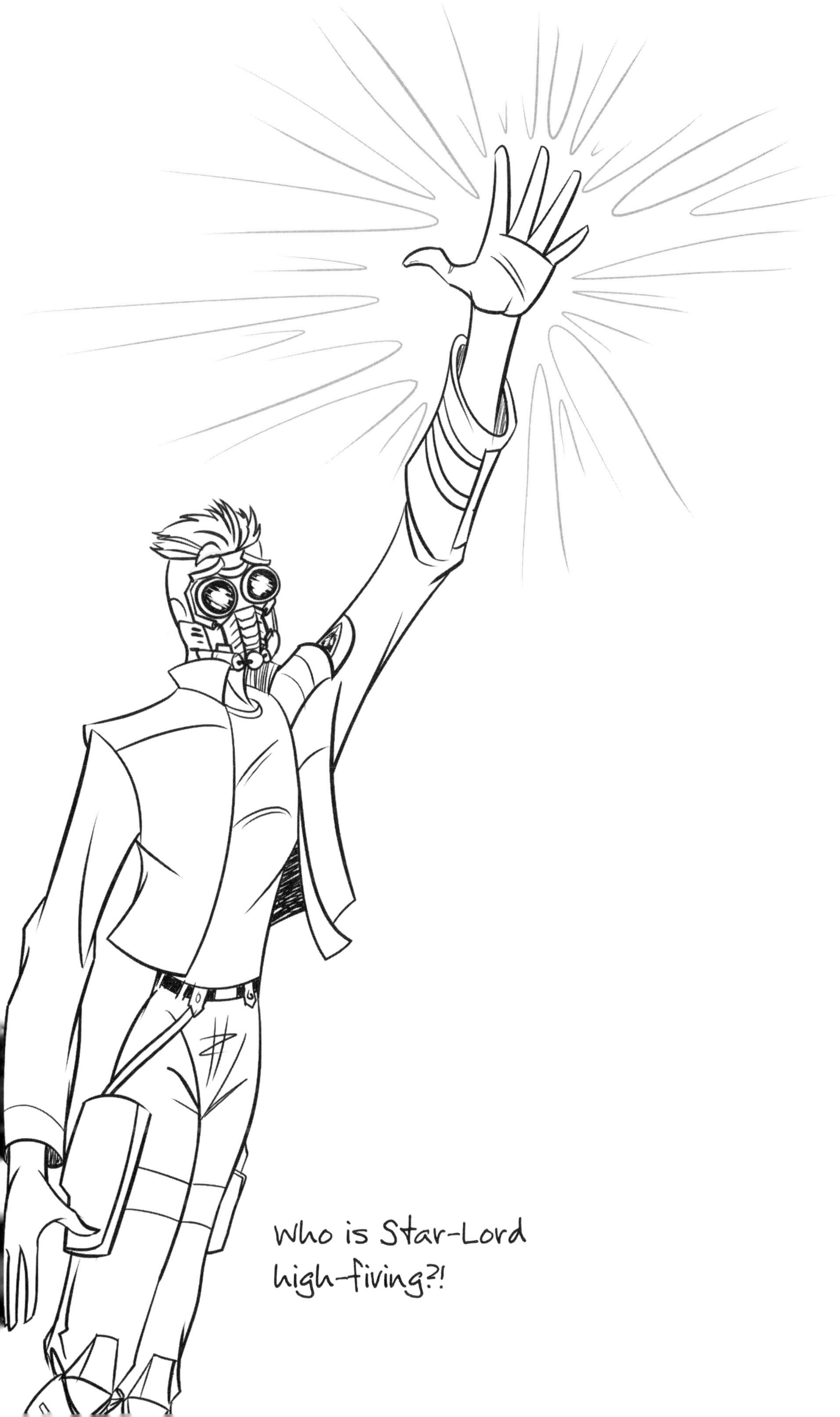

Who is Star-Lord
high-fiving?!

Drax is thinking about getting a new tattoo,
so he sketched a bunch of options. Some of them
are cool! Some of them are not so cool.
What do they look like?

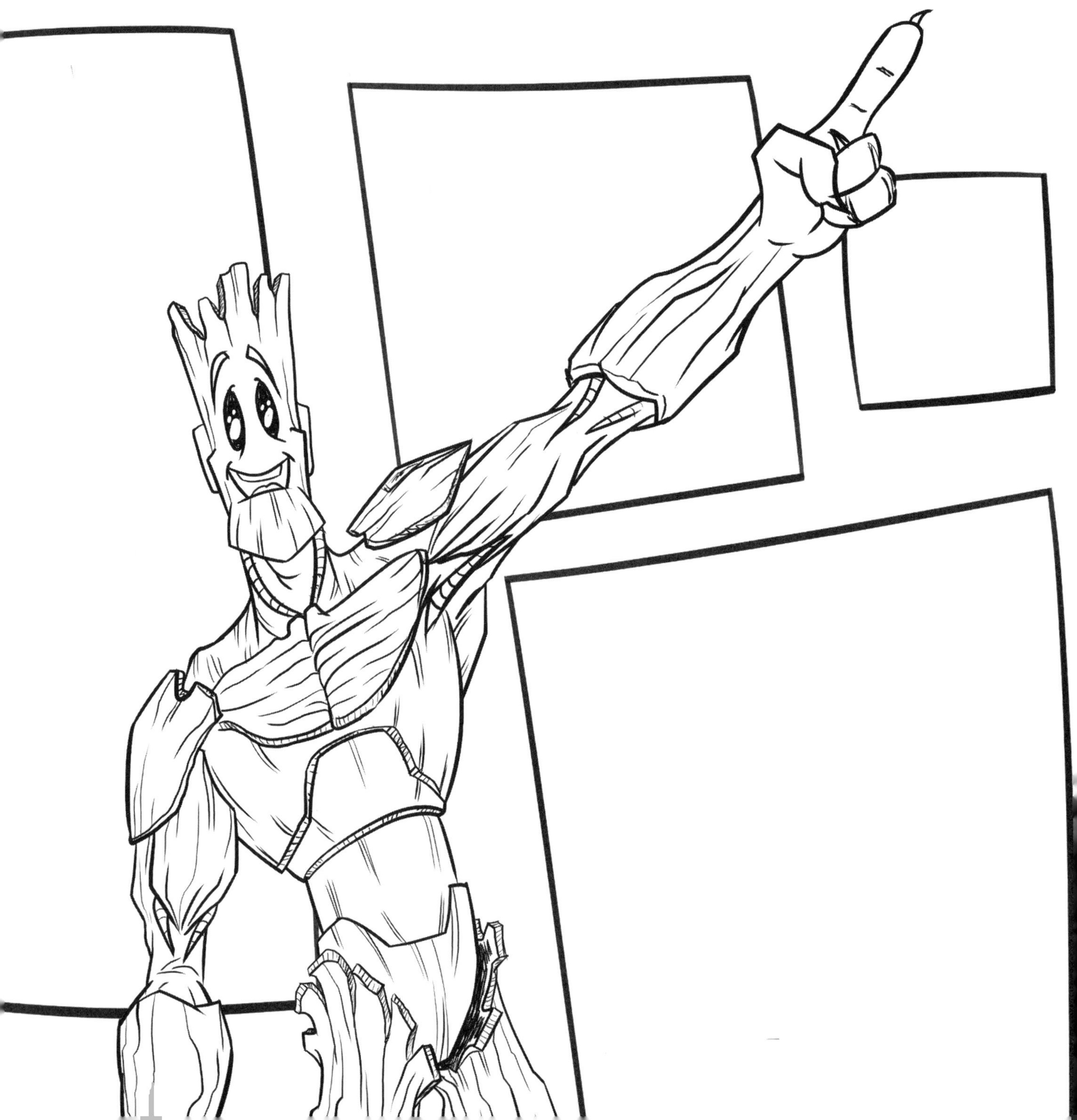

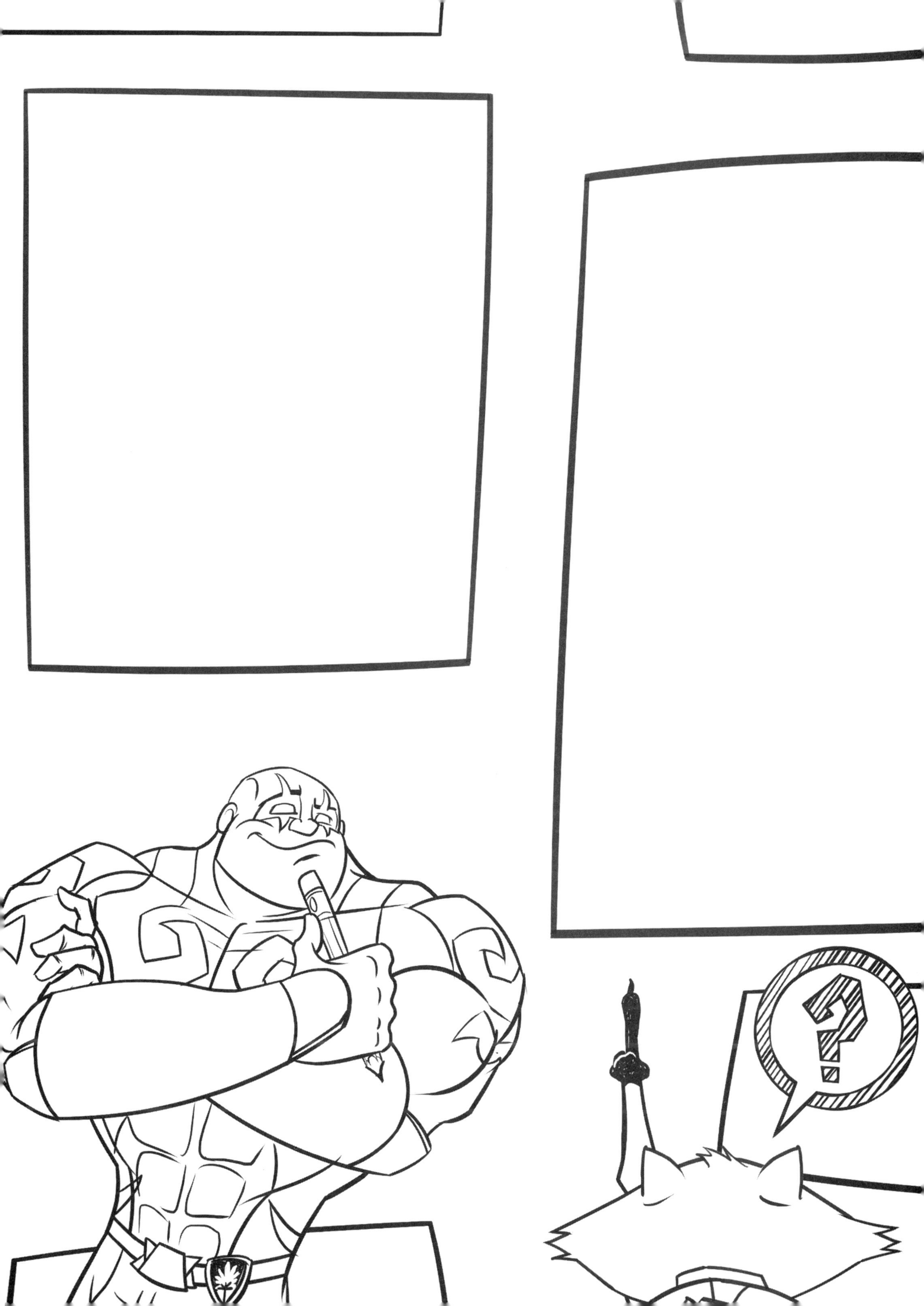

Star-Lord is totally beating Rocket at his favorite video game. DRAW IT!

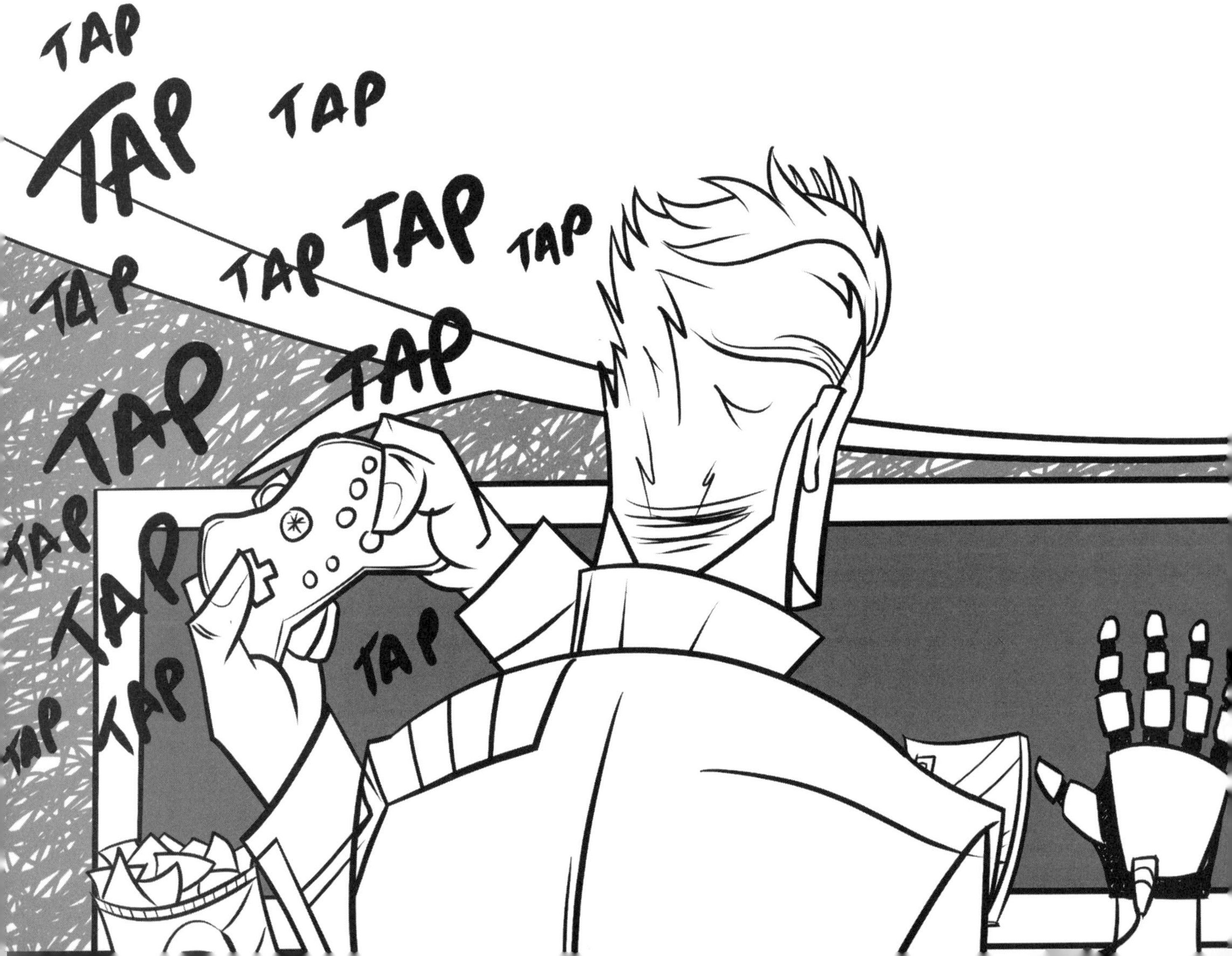
TAP
TAP
TAP
TAP
TAP
TAP
TAP
TAP
TAP
TAP
TAP
TAP
TAP
TAP
TAP

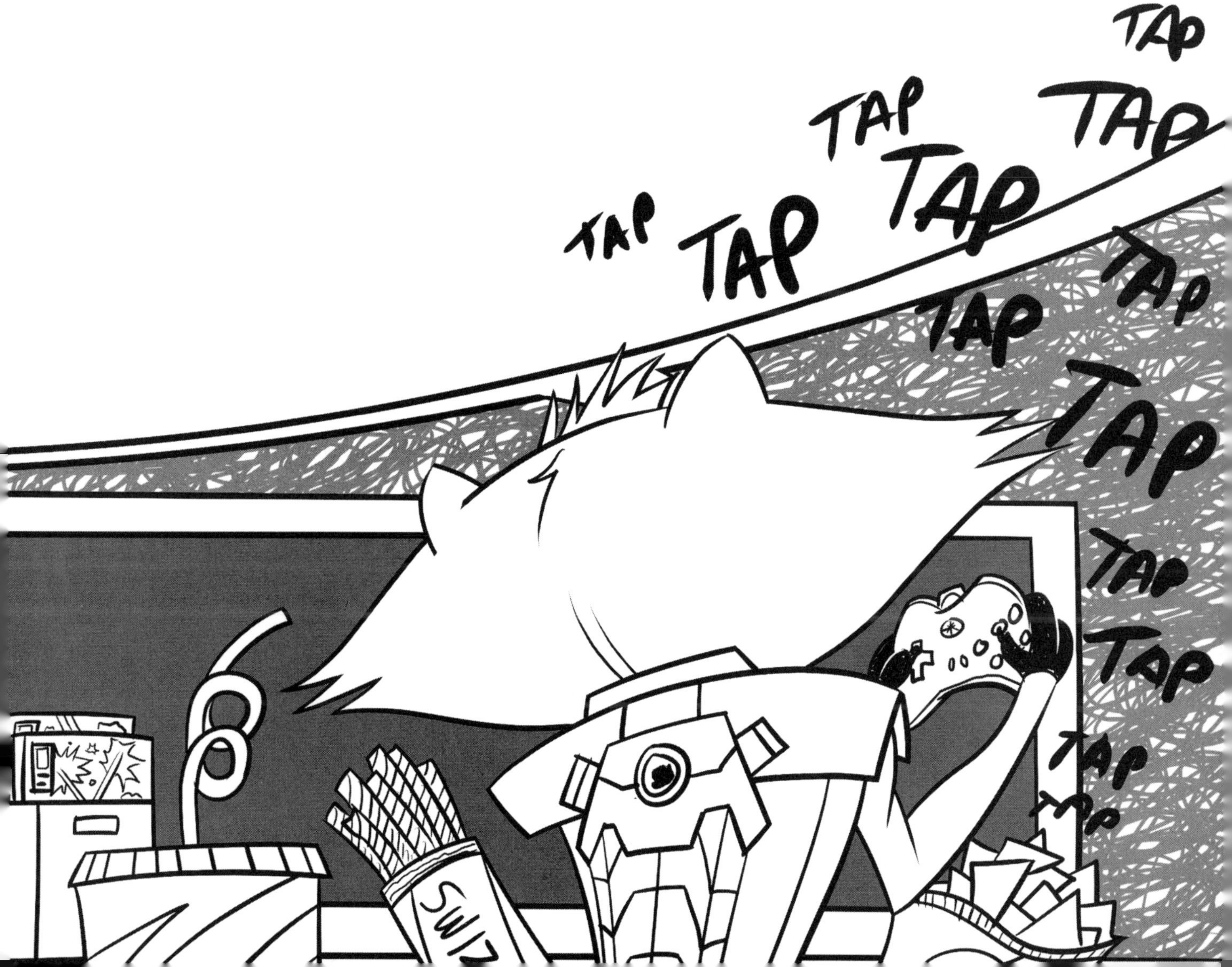
TAP
TAP
TAP
TAP
TAP
TAP
TAP
TAP
TAP
TAP
TAP
TAP
TAP

Drax the Destroyer needs a logo.
Draw one for him and make sure it captures
everything you need to know about how
cool he really is.

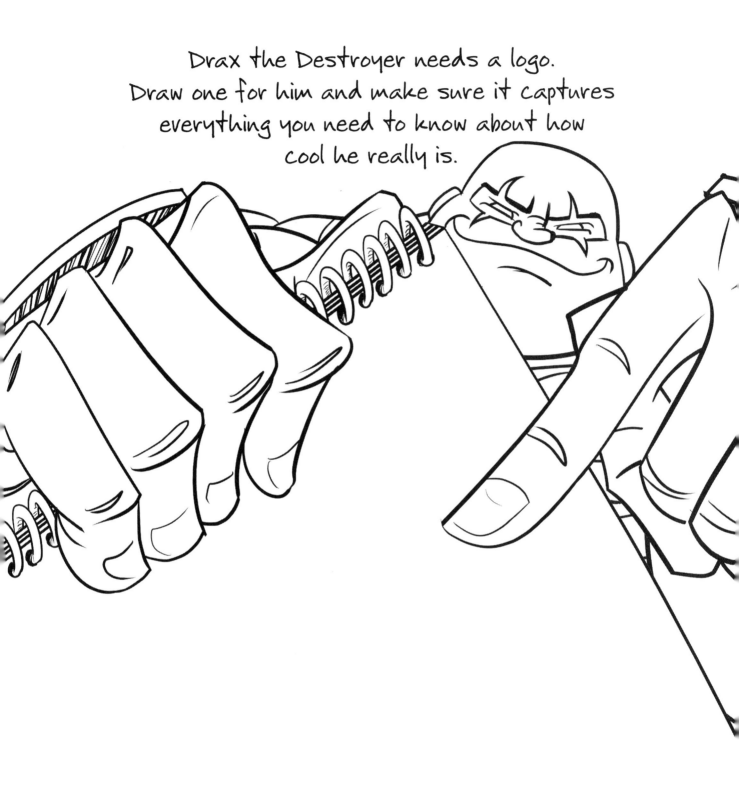

Rocket gave Groot a VERY
unique birthday present this year.
WHAT IS IT?!

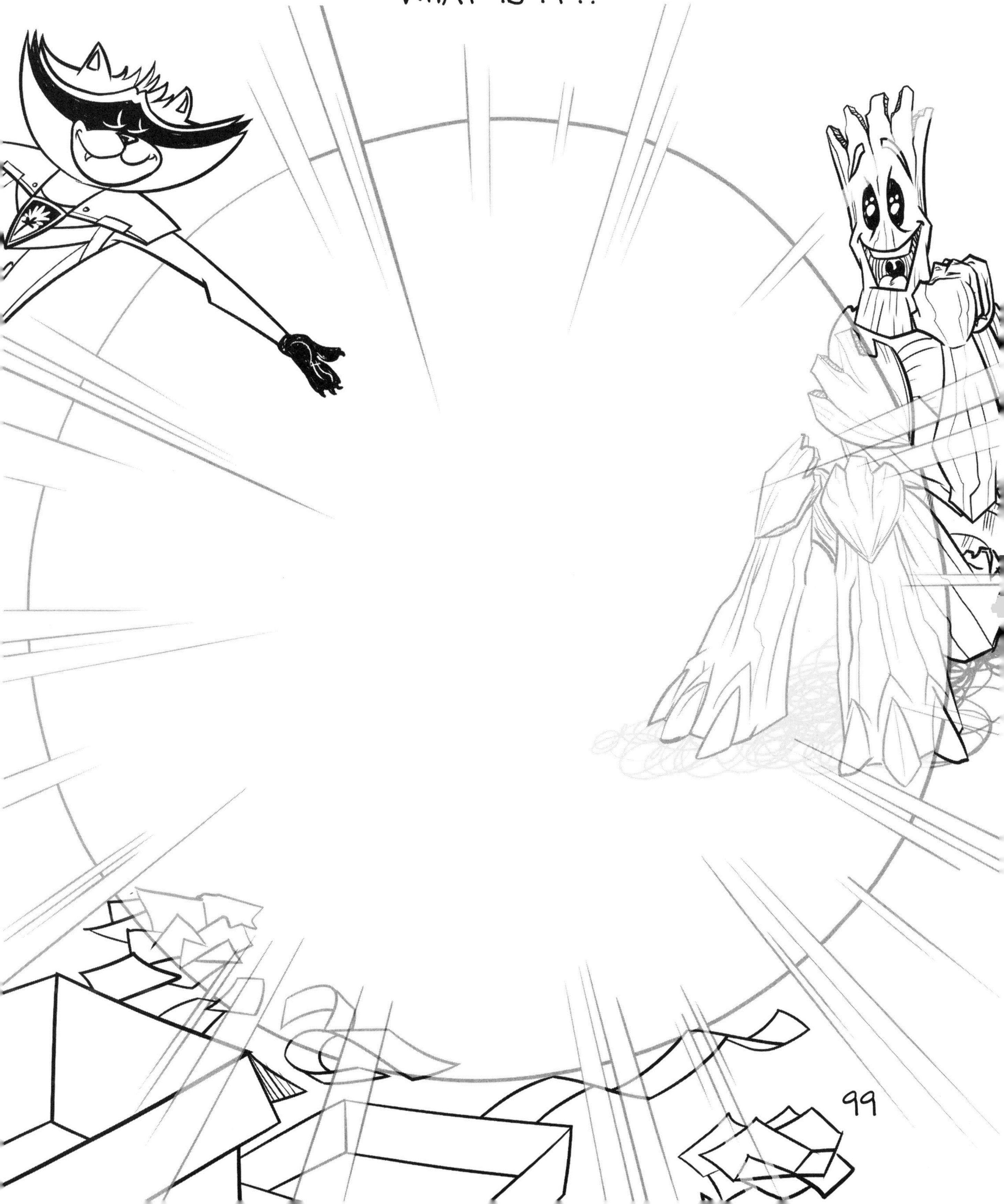

You don't need a crystal ball to predict what kinds of trouble the Guardians will find themselves in, but it always helps. Draw them a very strange fate.

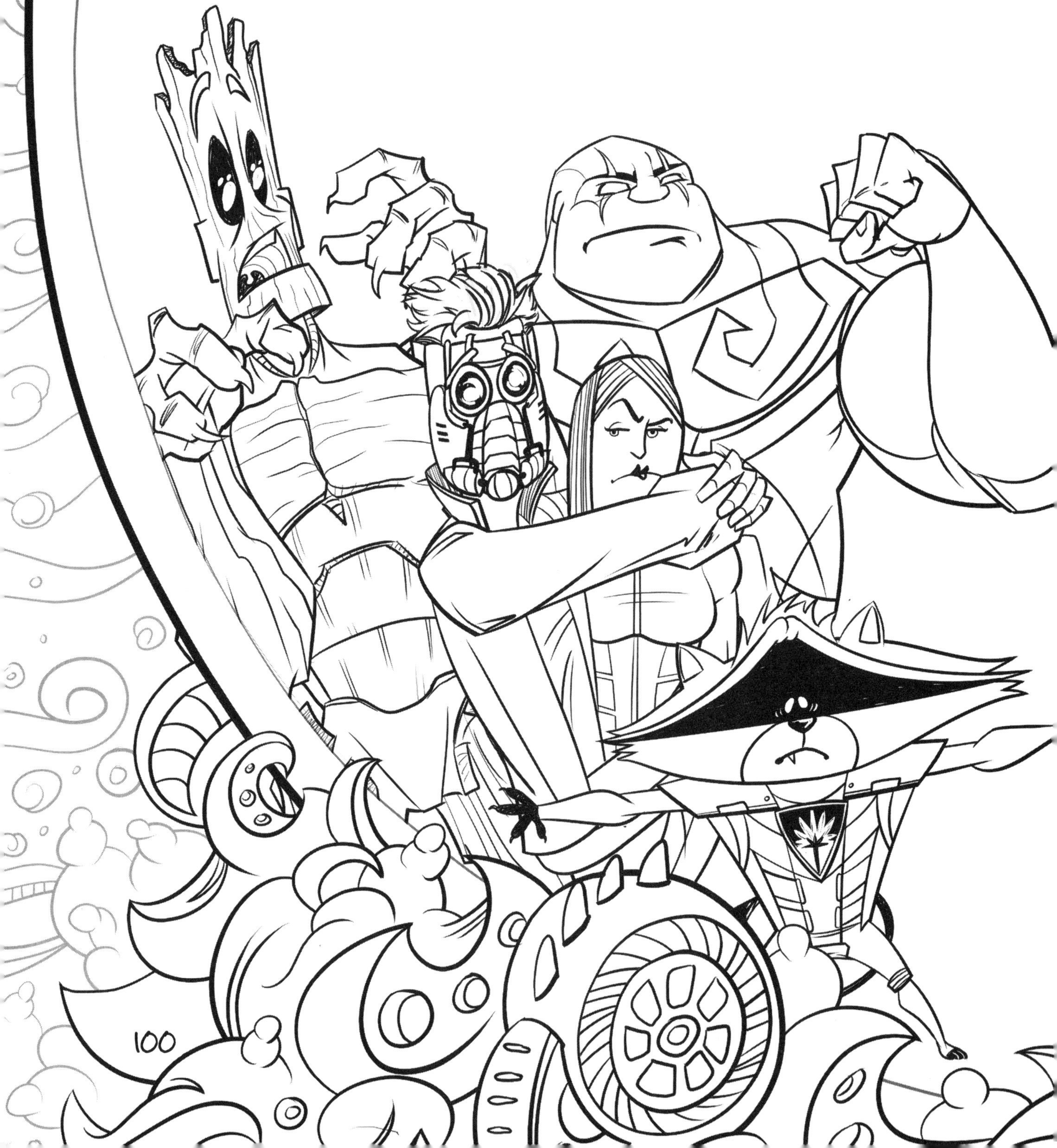

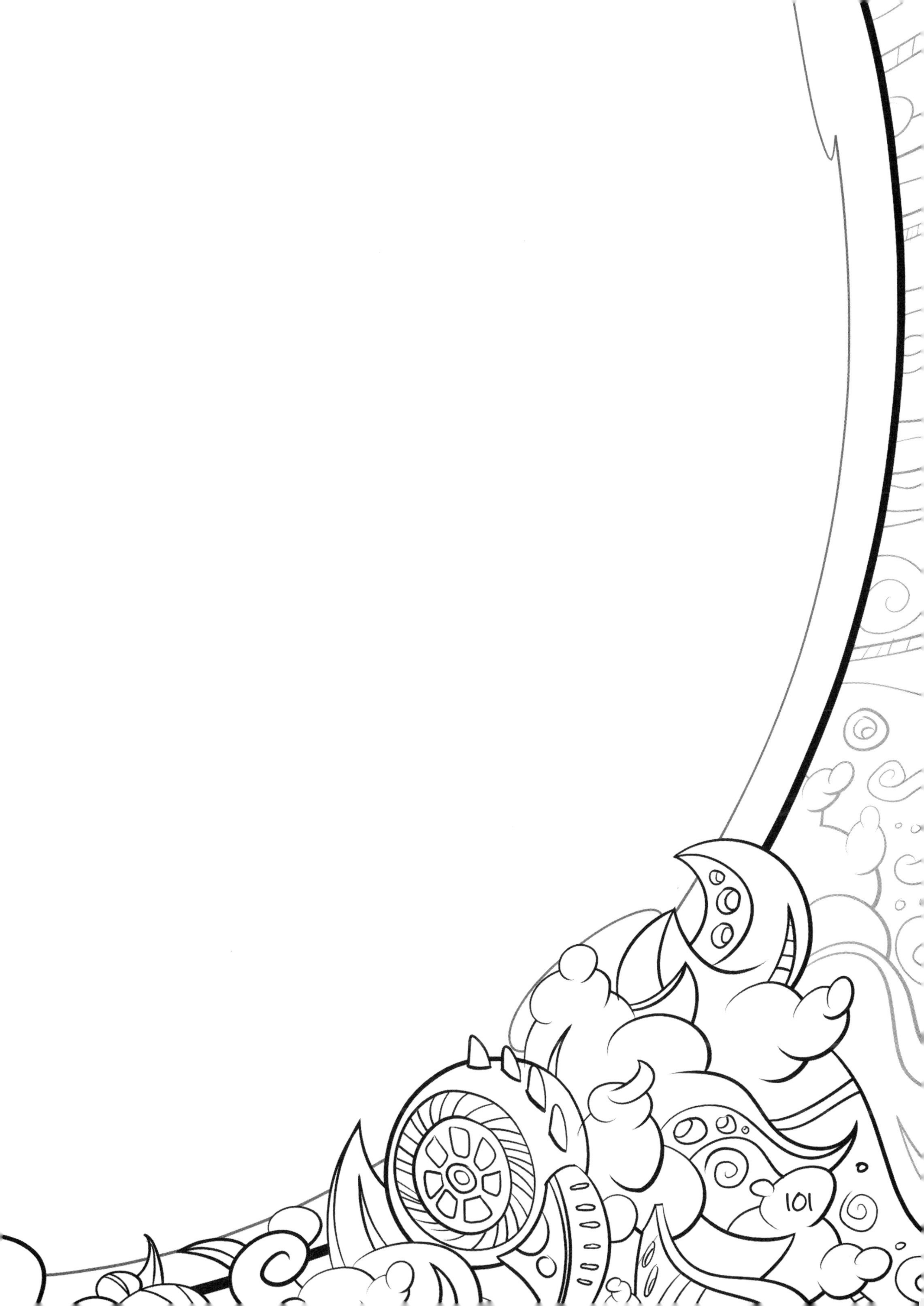

Star-Lord brought out the old photo album again. He's had a lot of good times with the Guardians, but he's had some freaky times, too. Draw a variety of scenes from the past.

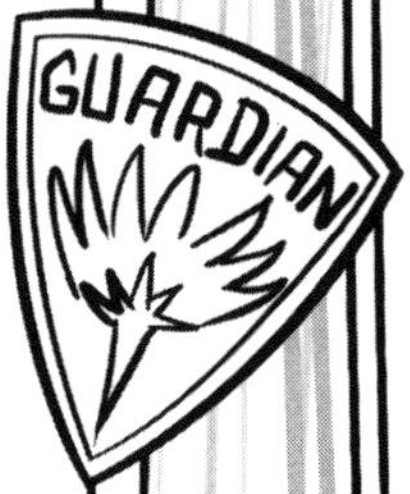
GUARDIAN

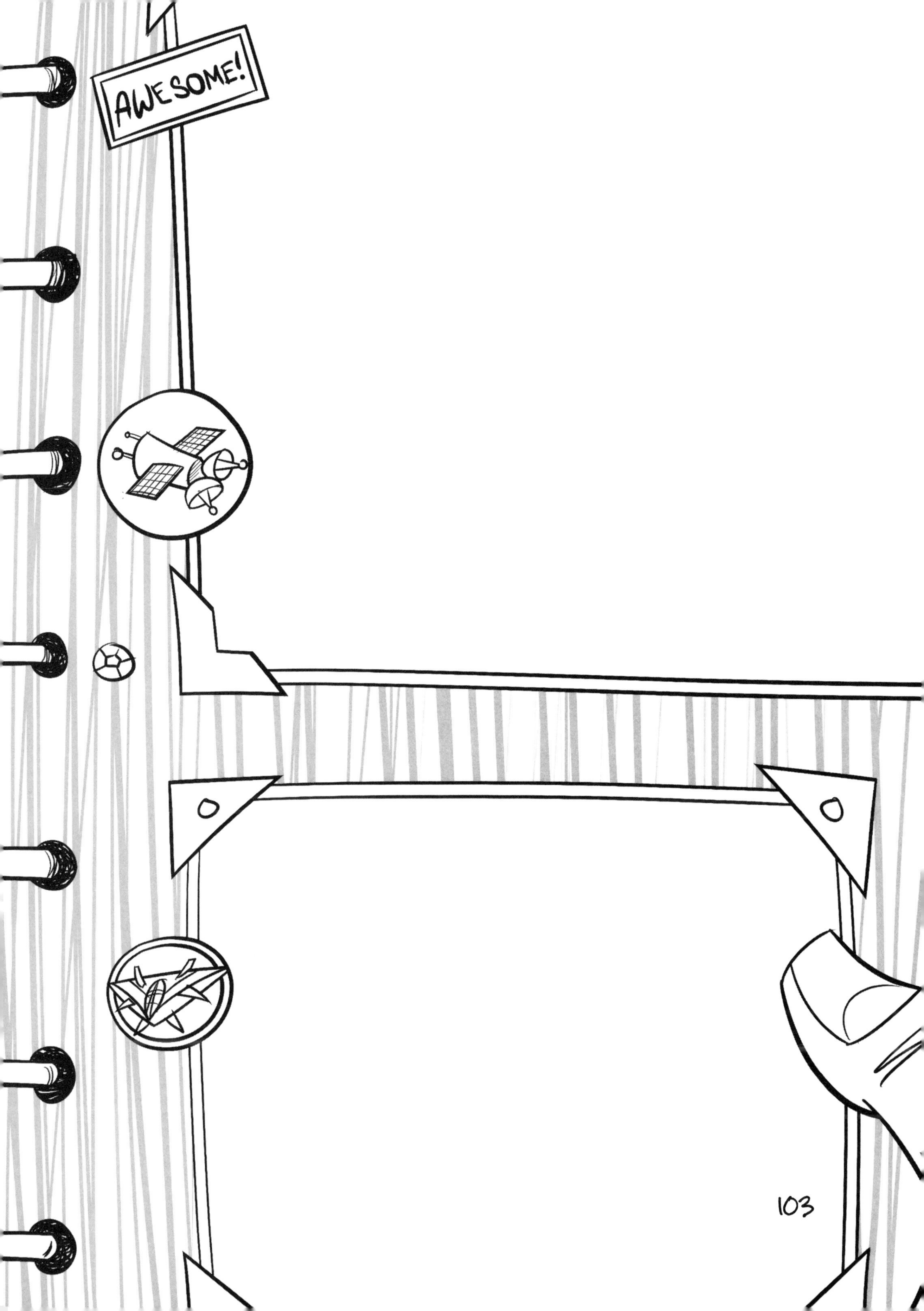
AWESOME!

What exactly is the Collector trying to sell?
Draw it!

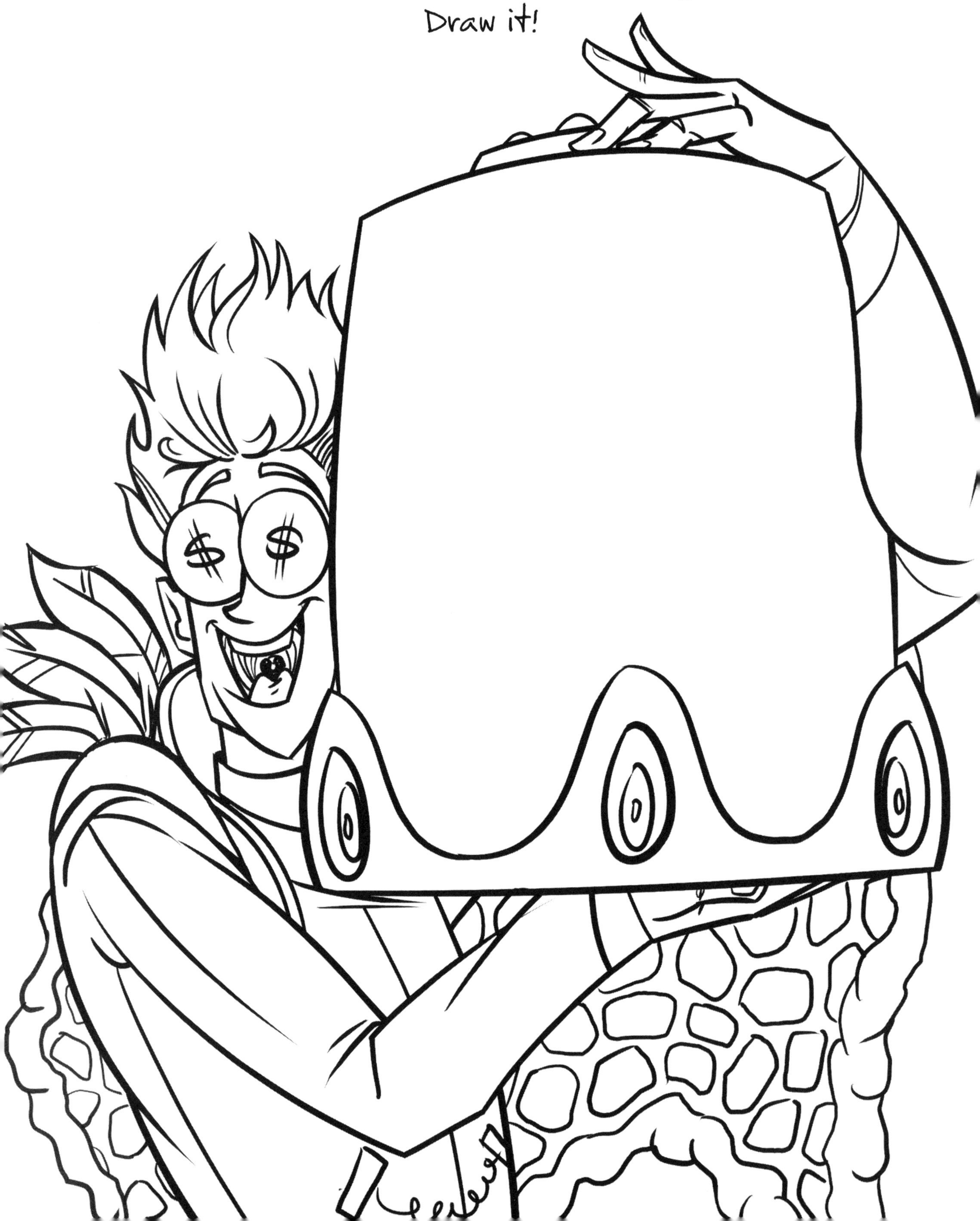

Star-Lord has got an awesome new mixtape, but it's missing something. Give it some cool designs.

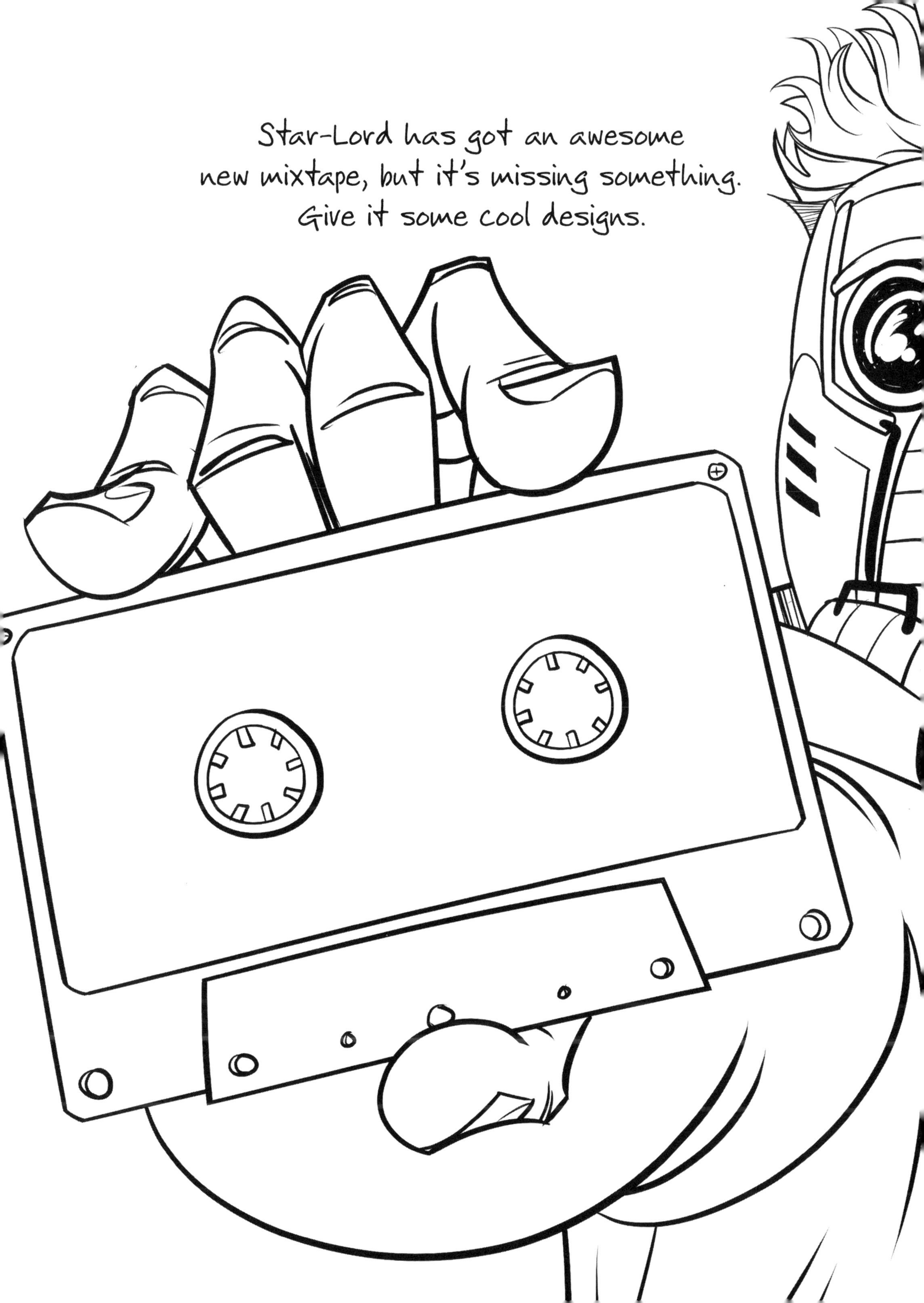

Drax's bowl of noodles is alive!
Draw some bugs and slugs
in his dinner.

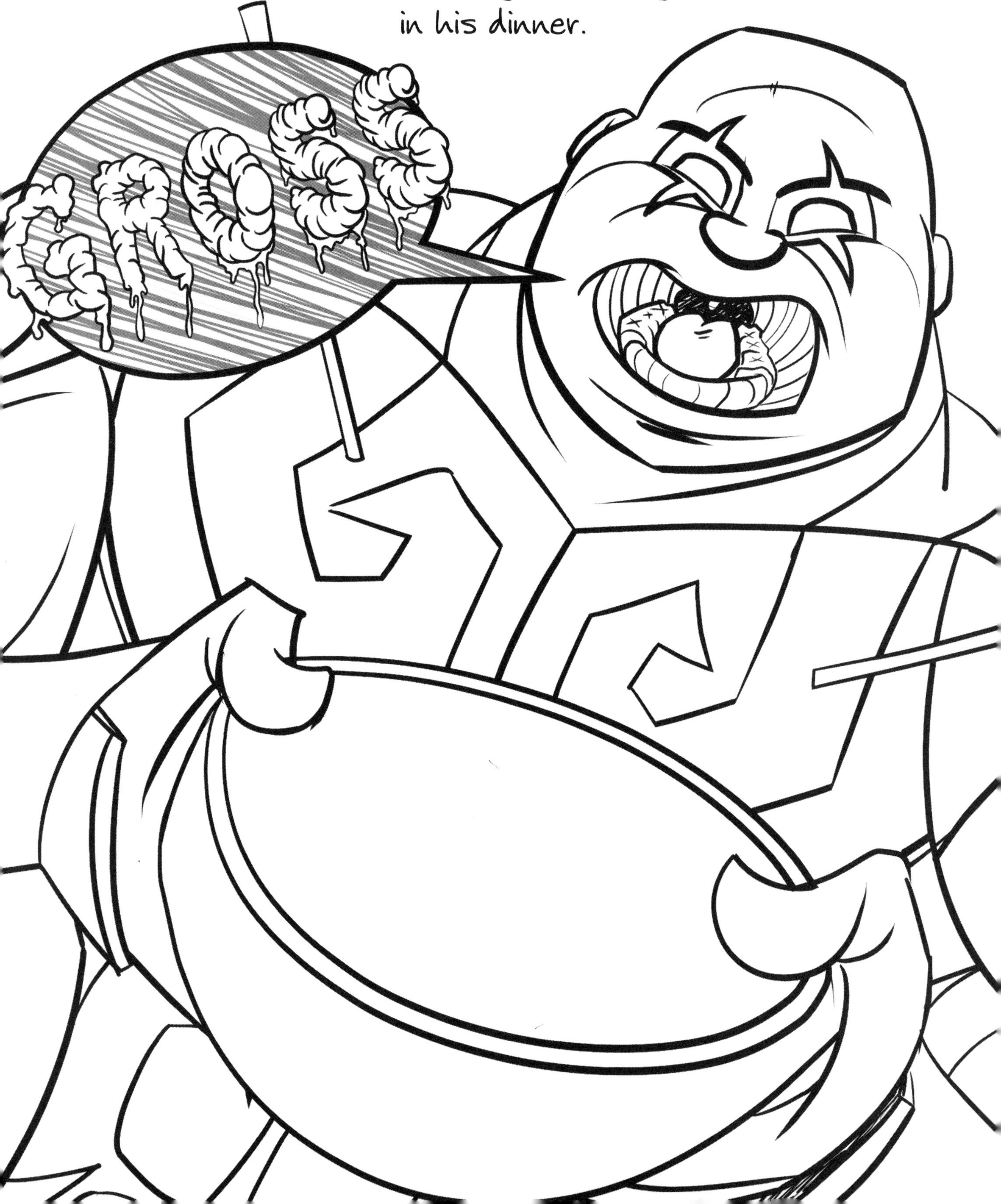
GROSS

Rocket is confused about
something he just can't seem to figure out.
Draw his peculiarly puzzled face.

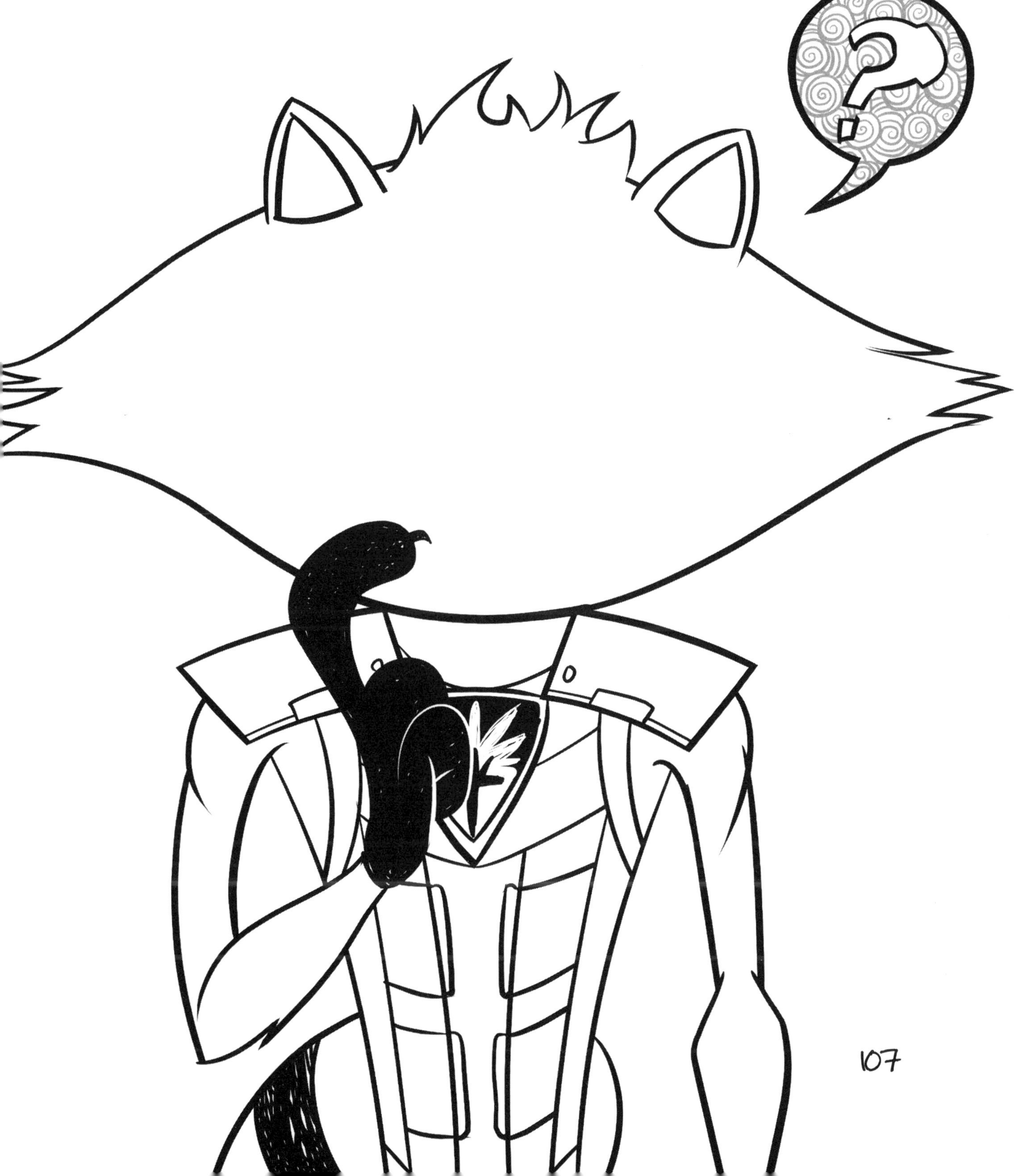
?

The Guardians have entered a strange video
game world where everything is pixelated.
Draw them as if they were made of tiny CUBES!

YOU MEAN LIKE THIS?

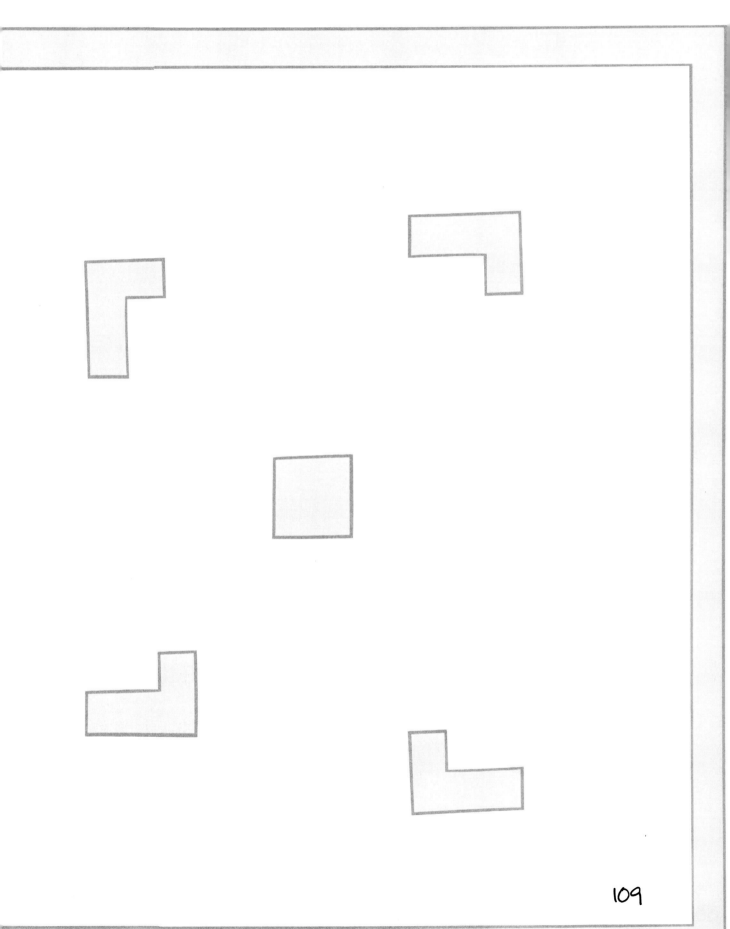

The Guardians just discovered a secret cavern on the planet Morag, and it's filled with stuff that will change the universe FOREVER! What kinds of things are inside it?

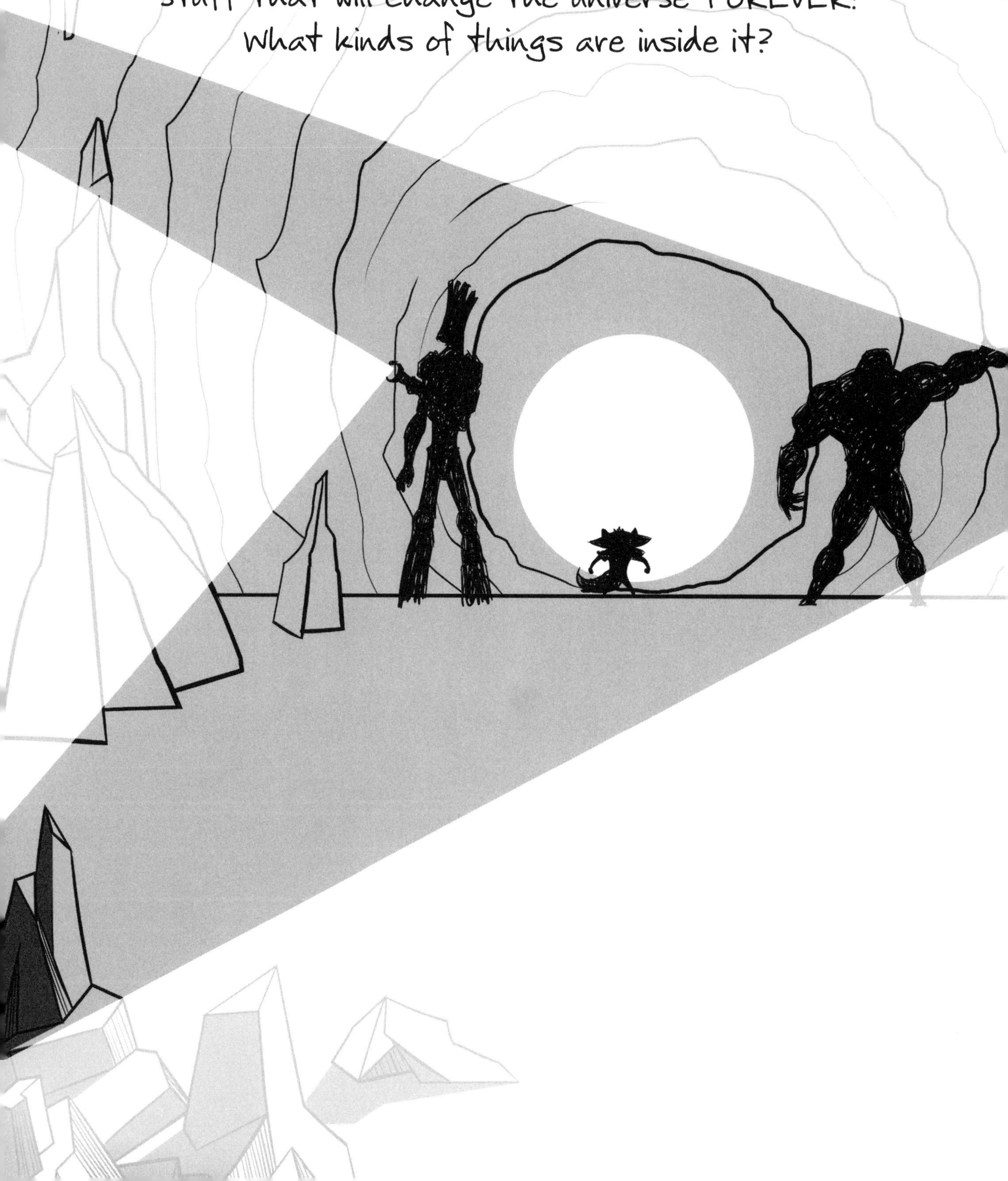

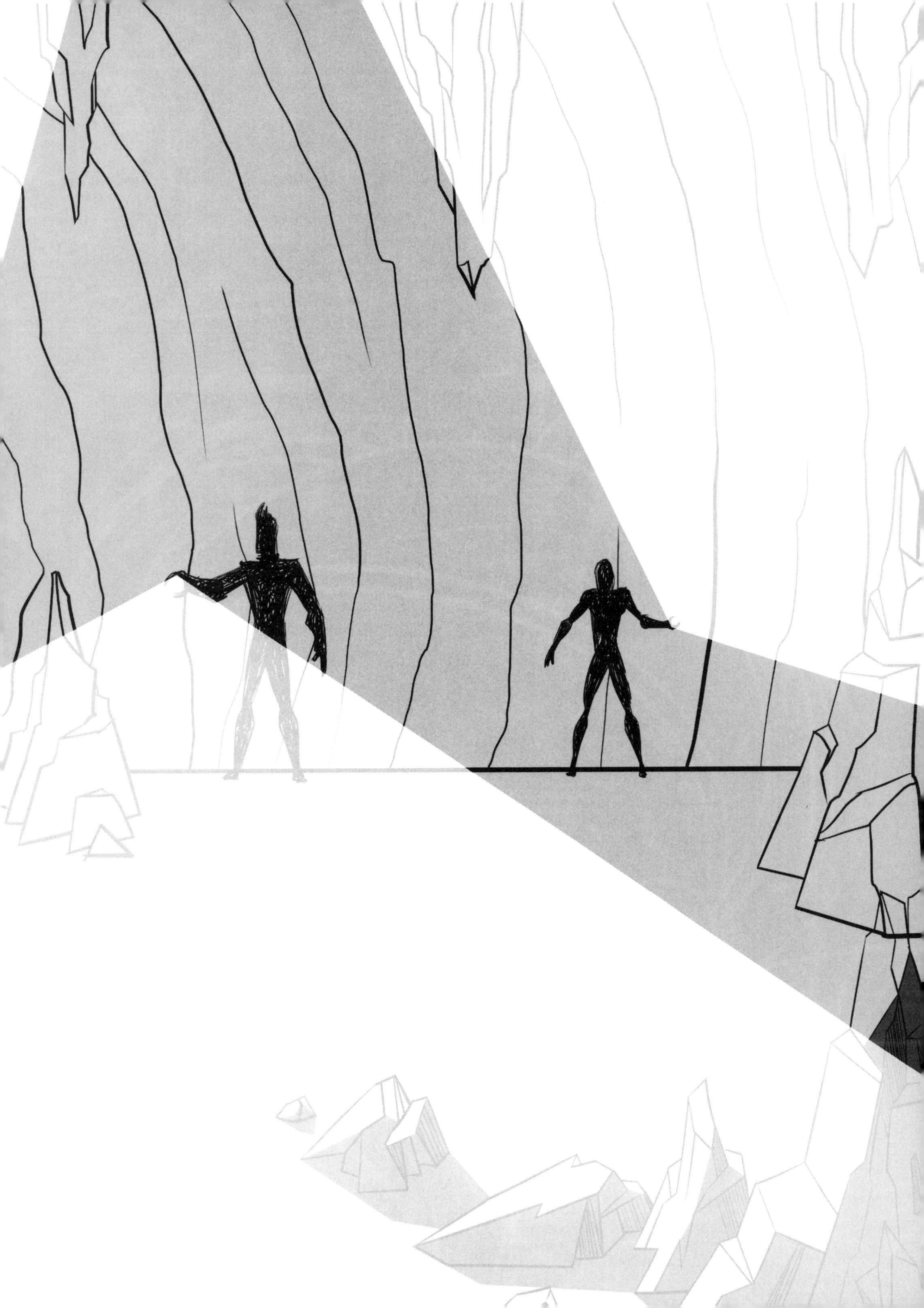

Star-Lord needs you to cover his jacket with really important awards and medals. He IS a lord of stars, after all.

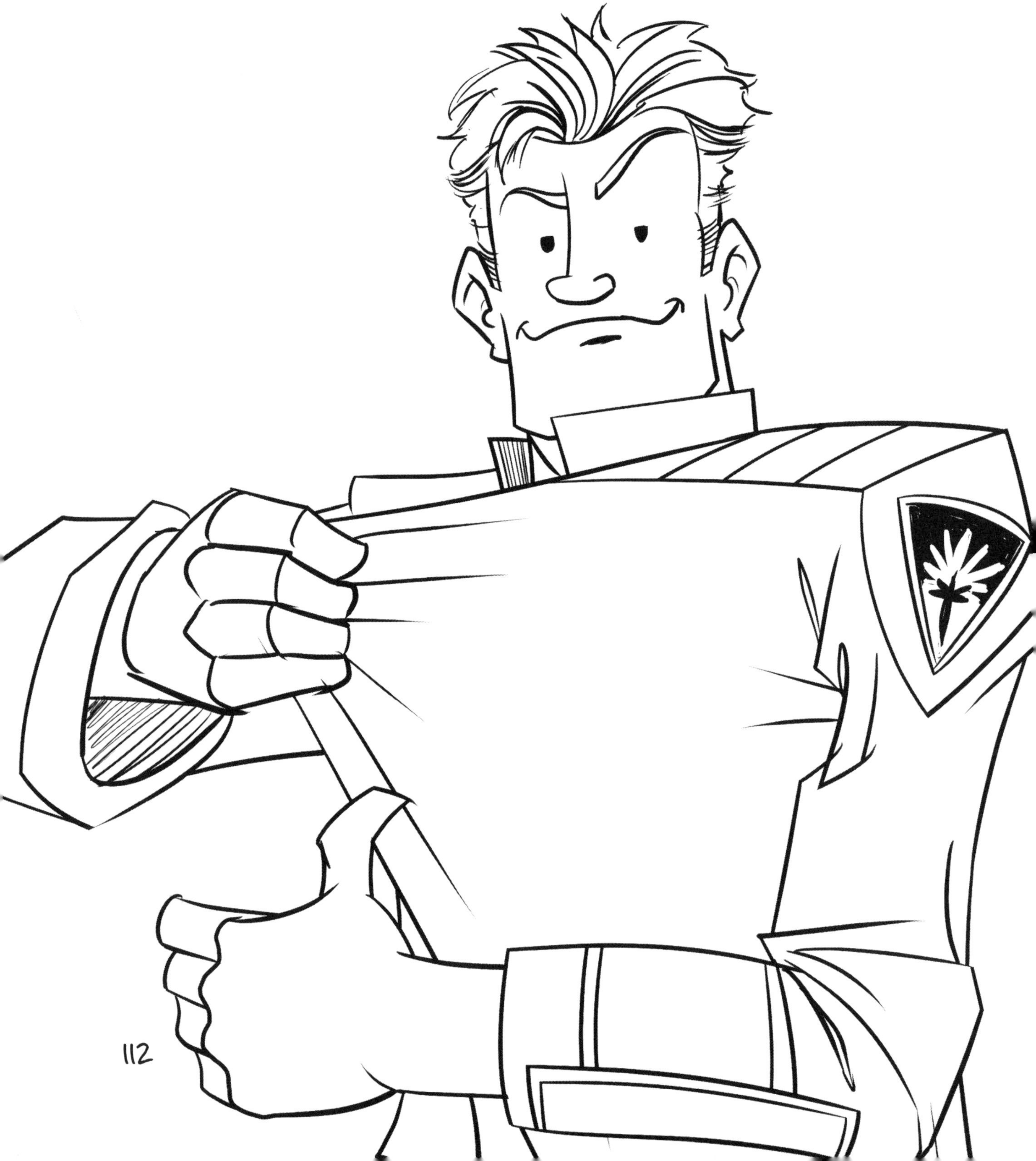

Drax just woke up and
is feeling really tired and grumpy.
Draw his grouchy face.

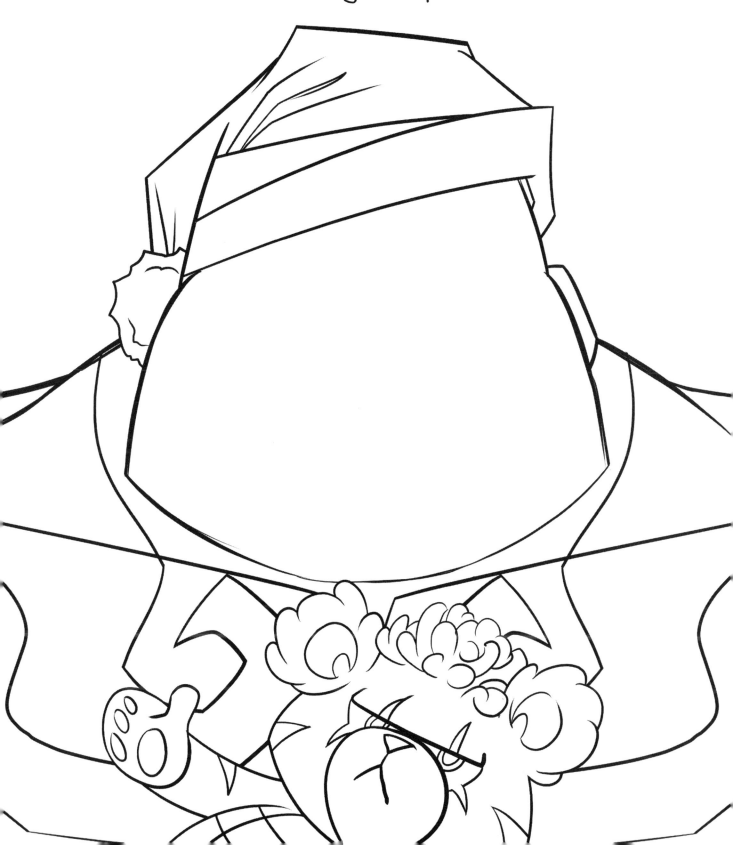

Rocket accidentally made a big group of alien bounty hunters angry. He does that A LOT.

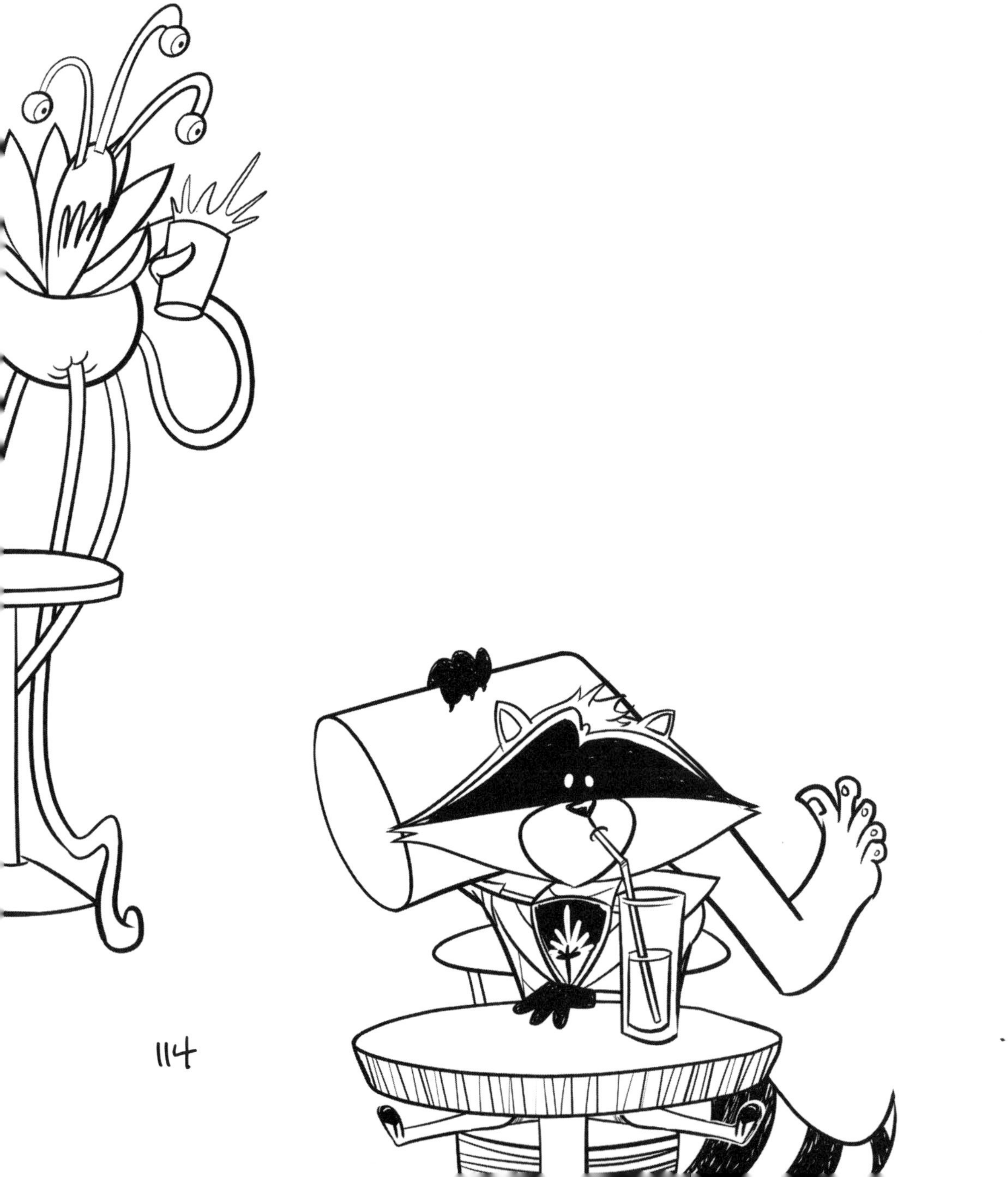

Draw a bunch of nasty-looking alien bad guys who
are ready to stomp all over him.

No one puts Gamora in a box! No one but YOU,
that is. What is she doing in this box, anyway?

Is Thanos thinking about kittens and rainbows?
That's entirely up to YOU!
Draw what you think is on his mind.

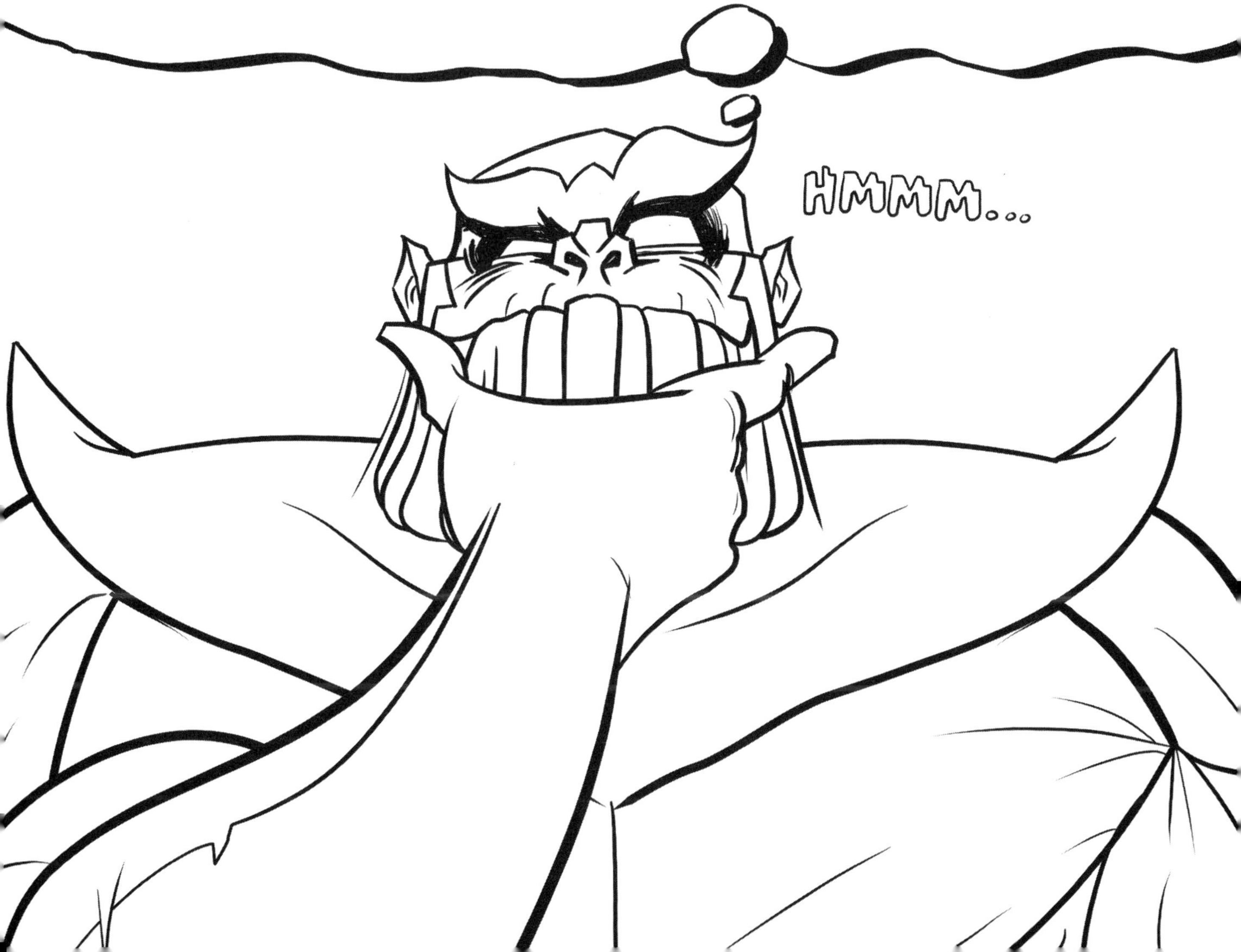
HMMM...

Groot created a battalion of stick warriors and
now he's sending them off to battle!
Draw a whole bunch of little stick people
who are ready to fight!

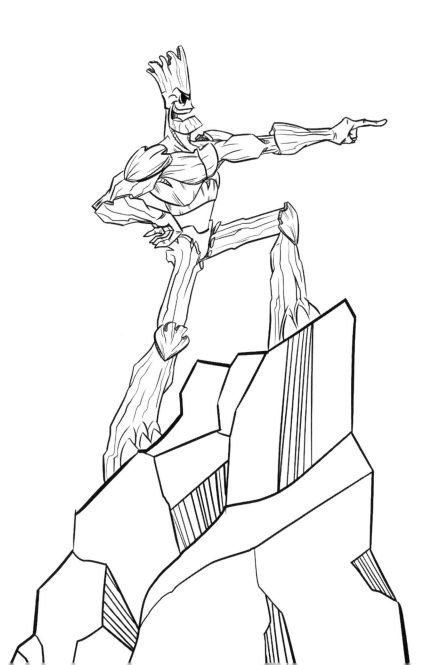

Star-Lord thinks he has a way with the ladies, but not this one.
Draw a big bad alien lady who isn't affected by his constant flirting.

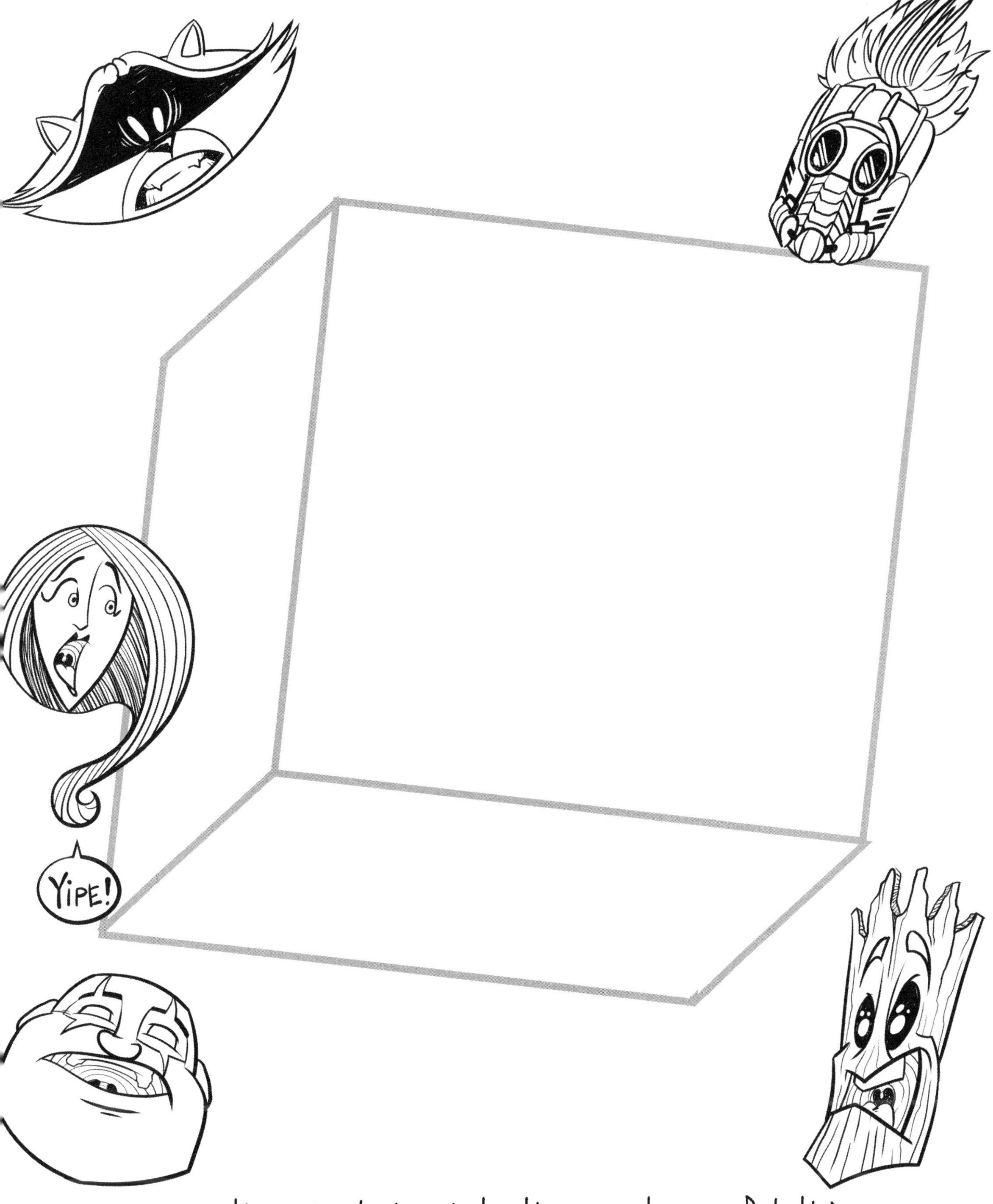
YIPE!

Turn this simple box into the most powerful thing in the entire galaxy. GO!

The Guardians are being confronted by visions of the future! What's going to happen to them? Draw it!

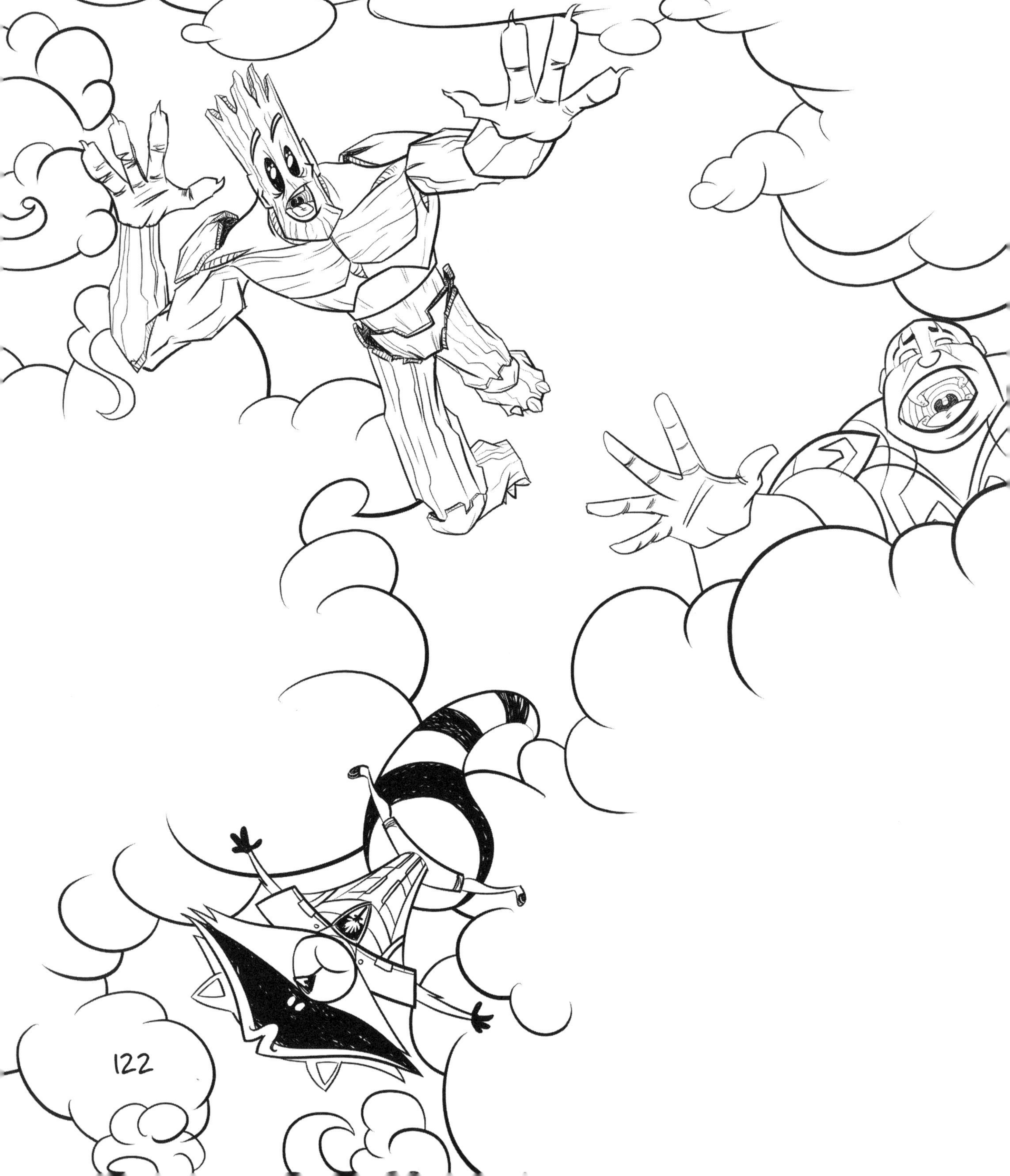

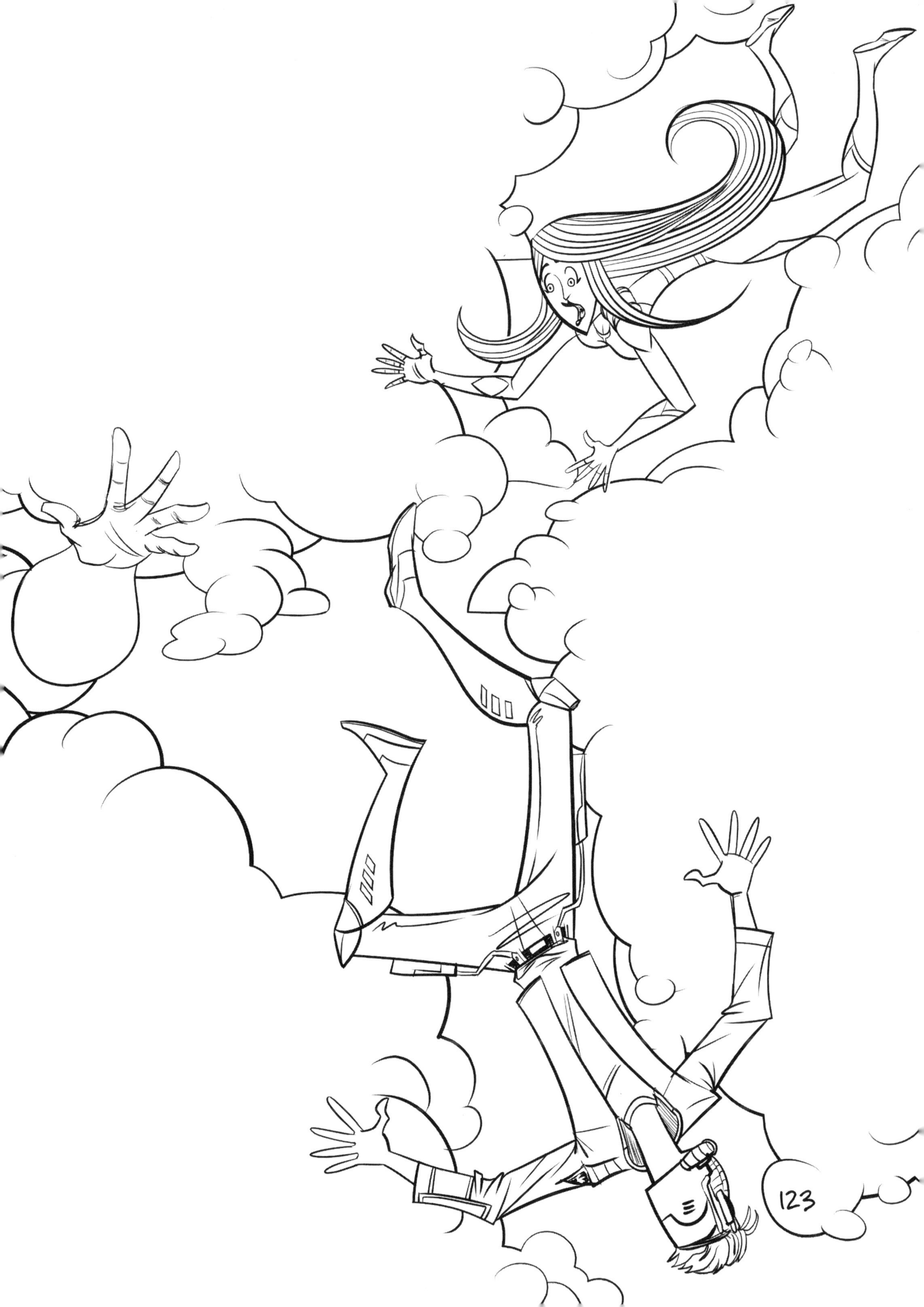

Groot is in bloom!
Draw a bunch of beautiful flowers
and plants on his tummy.

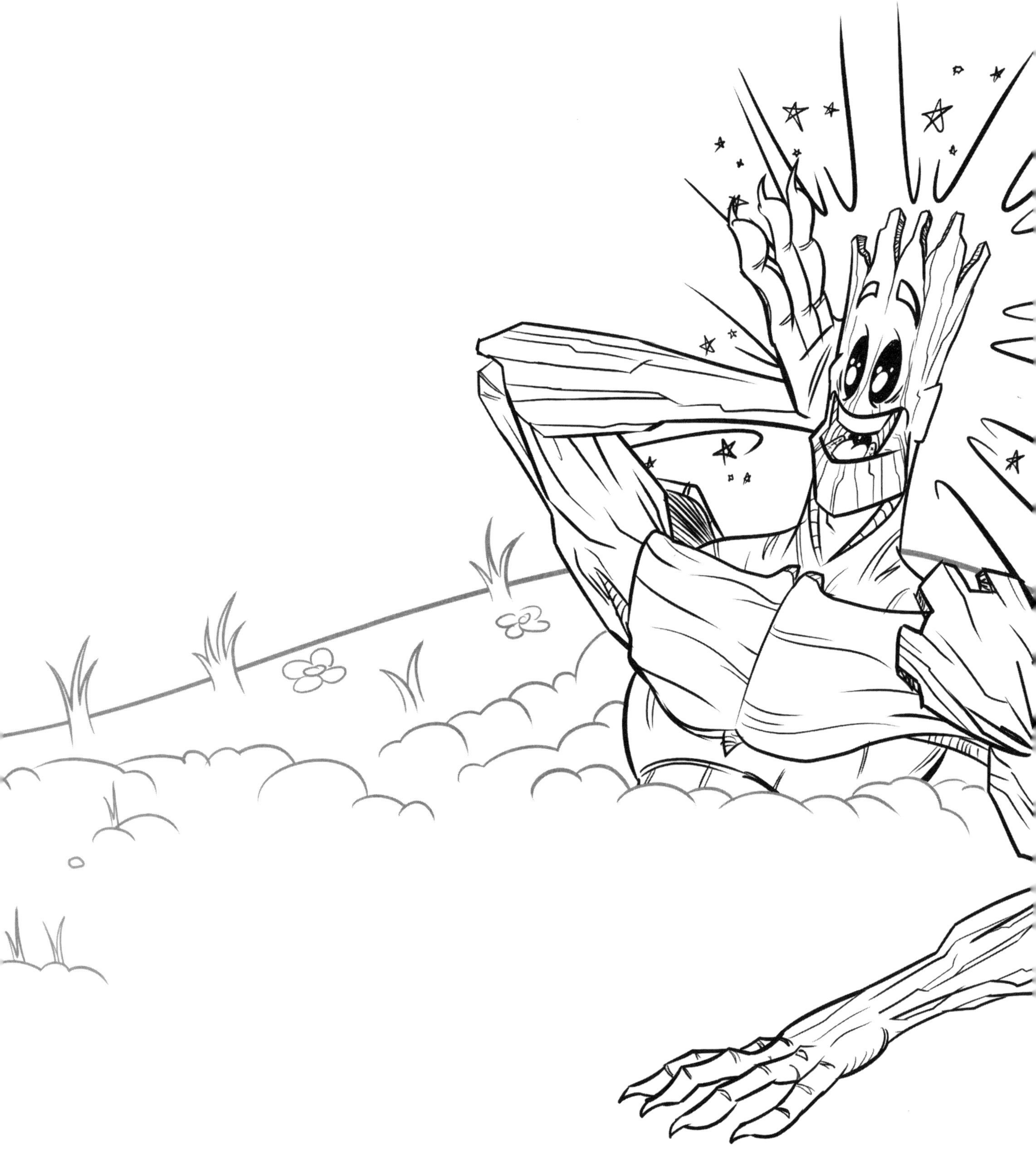

Fill this page with Rocket Raccoons.
Make them big, small, hairy, crabby, or stinky.
Draw A LOT of them.

Wouldn't it be funny if Gamora's arms
and legs were actually long, slimy tentacles?
Draw that!

What if Star-Lord wore a frilly dress?
DRAW THAT!

The Guardians of the Galaxy
have a BRAND-NEW member!
Is it YOU?

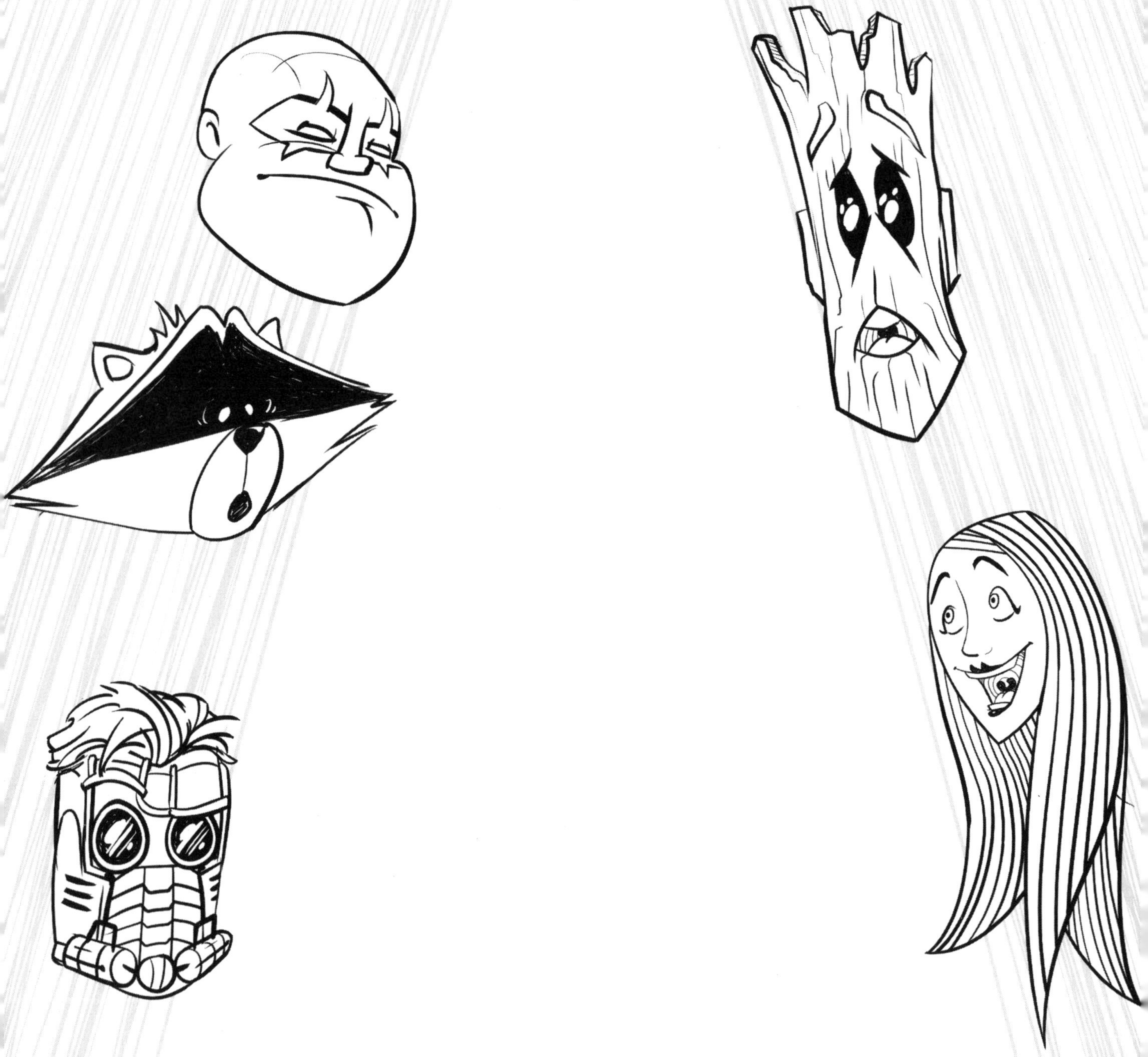